Olivia Kidney

By Ellen Potter

Illustrated by Peter Reynolds

SCHOLASTIC INC.

New York Toronto London Auckland Sydney
Mexico City New Delhi Hong Kong Buenos Aires

ISBN 0-439-63248-X

Text copyright © 2003 by Ellen Potter.
Illustrations copyright © 2003 by Peter H. Reynolds. All rights reserved.
Published by Scholastic Inc., 557 Broadway, New York, NY 10012,
by arrangement with Philomel Books, an imprint of Penguin Putnam Books for
Young Readers, a division of Penguin Group (USA) Inc. SCHOLASTIC
and associated logos are trademarks and/or registered trademarks of Scholastic Inc.

12 11 10 9 8 7 6 5 4 3 2 1   4 5 6 7 8 9/0

Printed in the U.S.A.   40

First Scholastic printing, March 2004

Designed by Gina DiMassi.

Text set in Worcester Round.

The art for this book was created on an Apple iBook with a Wacom graphics
tablet and light pen using Macromedia Flash.

For Adam, a very first-rate person.

–E. P.

For Lexxy.

–P. R.

One

Olivia Kidney's new home was an apartment building made of maroon and yellow bricks on New York City's Upper West Side. It was twenty-two stories high, and it contained some of the most awful people you'd ever want to meet. They crabbed up the elevators with their cold, unfriendly faces. The people who lived above her stomped on the floor if she was talking too loudly, and the people below her hit their ceiling with a stick if she was walking too loudly.

"I'm a human being!" Olivia had dropped to her knees, cupped her hands around her mouth, and called down through the floor. "I'm entitled to *move*! I'm not made of stone, you know!"

"Well, you walk like you are!" a muffled voice shouted up through her floor. Olivia's father, George Kidney, thought that was pretty funny. He had just taken the job as the apartment building's new superintendent. A new job for him and a new school for Olivia. In the past two years, Olivia had changed schools four times. The problem was that George, who was the absolute nicest man in the entire United States, and possibly Canada too, was a terrible superintendent. If he did manage to fix someone's showerhead, you could be sure that the toilet would then overflow. If he installed someone's ceiling fan, it would come crashing down the next day like a crippled helicopter. Each time he was fired, he would have to find a new apartment building for him to superintend, and for him and Olivia to live in.

But this place . . . this place was the worst yet.

It was November and cold as heck. Olivia stood outside the building, fumbling through her knapsack for her keys. Usually she kept her house keys clipped to a hook on the outside of her knapsack. But today they weren't there. She figured she had absentmindedly tossed them into her knapsack that morning. Now she pulled off her glove so that her fingers could wade through all the garbage—gum wrappers, five exploded pens, a book on séances called *Chatting With Ghosts* that she had stolen from her brother's bookshelf, a used Band-Aid, a loose-leaf notebook, and an old door chain that her father had given her and that she thought she might turn into a charm bracelet. Her fingers searched for the jagged shape of keys while an icy wind slapped at her ears and made her head hurt. Even her lips ached from the cold, and she tucked them in her mouth for warmth. She dug deeper into her knapsack, pawing around.

Nothing. A woman with a black fur Russian hat on her head and a face like an irritated ferret came up to the door, jangled her keys loudly as if to make a point, then opened the lobby door.

"Oh, thank you! Just in time!" Olivia said, her breath coming out of her mouth in cold, blue smoke. "I can't feel my toes anymore." But the woman slipped through the open door, then pulled it shut in Olivia's face.

"Strangers need to buzz up," she called through the door, pointing at the intercom buttons.

"I'm not a stranger!" Olivia called back. But the woman had already turned her back and walked away. "I'm not a stranger," Olivia muttered to herself. "It's just that no one here knows me." She wished that her brother, Christopher, was here. She never minded things too much as long as he was with her.

Olivia buzzed 12C once, knowing full well that her father wouldn't be home to buzz her in. The building was so large that he was always off fixing something. With luck, Olivia thought, he was also messing something up. Then he could get fired, and they could get out of this place as quickly as possible.

When no one buzzed her in, she sighed. In front of the building was a large concrete planter with two threadbare saplings in the center. Olivia sat down on the low barrier and resumed the search for her keys. On the street in front of her a large group of children was playing freeze tag, a perfect game for the day's weather. They were screaming and laughing. One skinny, freckled girl was sitting on the concrete bench watching, bundled in a coat that was too large for her, and screaming with them. They probably all lived in the building. They probably all had keys. Olivia hated them.

She turned her knapsack inside out, let all her stuff fall in a pile on the pavement, and stared at it: No keys. Great, just great. She picked up the séance book and started to put it back in the knapsack.

"They don't work in general." The voice came from behind her. She straightened up and turned. It was a boy with no shoes on. He was standing there, on the freezing cold sidewalk, in his socks. The socks were not very clean either, and a hole was threatening on his right big toe. He gave off the faint odor of a barnyard.

"Séances . . . you know, trying to contact dead people," the boy said, pointing to Olivia's book. "They don't generally work."

"Do you live in this building?" Olivia asked. The boy nodded.

"I'm in your English class at school," he said. Olivia was surprised that anyone in her class would know who she was. She had arrived at the new school in the middle of the term. Everyone had already paired up into best friends or airtight cliques. Story of her life! The only time they seemed to notice Olivia was when she left early to go to her appointment with Ms. Dart. Then a few of them would stare or whisper to each other about her.

"My name is Branwell Biffmeyer," the boy said. "I sit next to Wayne."

"Wayne? Oh, you mean that kid with the thing?" Olivia asked, scrunching up her nose.

"It's a boil," Branwell said defensively. He was a tall, sturdy-looking boy with dark, heavy-lidded eyes and dark brown hair. His hands were rough; the skin on his fingertips had hard yellow calluses. He looked like he ought to be off playing sports somewhere. She didn't recognize him at all.

"Why don't you go off and play something," Olivia said, her eyes stinging from the cold.

"I would, but it's my turn to give up my shoes," he said.

"What?"

"There are eleven kids in my family and only ten pairs of shoes. It was my turn to give up my shoes." Olivia looked at the group of kids playing tag. They were of all different ages and sizes. They were all fabulously freckled.

"You mean those are all your brothers and sisters?" Olivia cried.

"Yup," said Branwell.

Olivia was moderately in awe. She herself had only one brother, Christopher, who was eight years older than her. She squinted. "How many bathrooms do you have?" she asked.

"Just one," said Branwell. Olivia nodded knowingly.

"You'll be meeting my father pretty soon then," she said, and she began to stuff the rest of her things back into her knapsack.

Then she remembered something. Today, when she had been leaving English class to see Ms. Dart, one of the boys had yanked her backward by her knapsack. "Freak," he had hissed at her. "Freaks go down to Ms. Dart." Olivia had heard something drop to the floor. Now she realized that the boy had probably yanked the keys right off their hook. But at the time her face was beet red with anger and embarrassment. She hadn't even turned around. In fact she didn't even look to see who the boy was—for all she knew, it might have been Branwell Biffmeyer.

"You look cold," Branwell said.

"Bug off," Olivia told him.

"Why don't you go inside?"

"Well, I would if I *could*. But my keys are gone, thanks to *some*body." She raised her eyebrow at Branwell to see if he reacted with any guilt. But he only smiled and reached into the collar of his shirt. He pulled out a leather necklace with three keys attached to a ring. She noticed his hands again. She had never seen such rough hands. She wondered if he could feel anything through all the thickened skin. He opened the door for her and followed her into the building.

"All right," Olivia said. "Thank you." She started toward the elevators and heard his socked feet padding behind her. She turned. "Bye now."

"How are you going to get into your apartment?" he asked. Good point. She hadn't thought of that. Inside, Branwell's barnyard odor was stronger.

She punched the elevator button. The elevators here took forever to come . . . that was another thing she hated about this place.

"Don't worry about it," Olivia said.

"I worry about a lot of things," said Branwell. "That's just how I am. You can come to my house and wait." Olivia could imagine what his apartment must be like—a crazy whorl of kids and, from the smell of it, sheep.

"No thanks." She heard the promising wind of the elevator as it whooshed down the shaft. The elevator door opened and Olivia gratefully slipped inside.

"We live in 6D, if you need us," Branwell said before the door closed. Olivia didn't imagine that was going to be likely.

Two

The elevator stopped on three. It made a stomach-clenching bobble before its metallic door hissed open. Two girls walked in, laughing and talking in low, secretive tones. When they saw Olivia, they narrowed their eyes at her, as if she had deliberately been spying on them. One of them was very glamorous. She appeared to be about fourteen, just two years older than Olivia, but she looked like a woman already. She had creamy, pale skin, and one of her black eyebrows was plucked so that it arched up higher than the other.

"Push ten for us," she said to Olivia. Olivia pushed the button for the tenth floor. The other girl had a plump face with dull, stupid eyes and a wide, mean grin. She was grinning when she got on the elevator and she never stopped grinning. She grinned directly at Olivia, and it made Olivia so uncomfortable that she looked away and

stared up at the panel of numbered lights above the door. The girls whispered to each other again and then burst out laughing. They were staring at Olivia's pants.

"We're sorry," the glamorous girl said to Olivia. "It's just the cuffs on your pants. They're so big!"

Olivia looked down at her cuffs. Maybe they were a little large. She had never thought about the size of pant cuffs. Now she wished she had. But still, she tipped her head up defiantly and replied, "There's nothing wrong with my cuffs."

"Nothing except you could carry all your spare change in them," the glamorous girl said.

"And your schoolbooks," the other one added. The elevator door opened and the girls stepped out.

"And a toaster oven . . ." Olivia heard their voices fade away down the tenth-floor hallway.

Olivia got out on the twelfth floor. It smelled of cooked onions. Over the years, Olivia had noticed that every floor in an apartment building has its own unique odor. In the last building she'd lived in, her floor smelled of old man's feet. Another floor she had lived on smelled like the juniors' department in Macy's.

Apartment 12C was at the far end of the hallway. She pressed the doorbell just in case her father had come home.

No one answered. Olivia took off her coat and slid down to the floor. She'd just have to wait. At least it was warm in here. But her stomach was growling something fierce.

Why couldn't her father have a *normal* job and be home at *normal* hours?! The fact that she'd lost her keys was *his* fault really, when you thought about it. If he hadn't always been getting fired from his jobs, Olivia wouldn't have had to go from school to school. And if she hadn't always been the new kid in school, people wouldn't have done nasty things to her—like swipe her keys. She decided then and there that when he did come home today, she was going to give him the Silent Treatment. He really hated that. "But Sweetpea," he would say, "we used to be pals, didn't we? Don't shut me out. We need each other now more than ever." He'd get all sad and flustered. Olivia wished he'd just get mad at her, but he never did.

She opened her knapsack and pulled out the book on séances. It was written by a woman named Madame Brenda. It was a very old book with a crackly binding. On its cover was an ink drawing of three people sitting around a table, holding hands. Floating above them, over their heads, was a man in a smoking jacket and a bowler hat. No one saw him because they all had their eyes shut. Olivia made a mental note to always keep her eyes open during a séance.

The first chapter of the book was full of warnings. It told of all the bad things that could happen if you didn't conduct your séance properly. It seemed that dead people could be quite ornery about being disturbed. If you didn't summon them in the right way, they might pinch your leg or tackle you to the floor. Then there were the boring dead people. If you had the misfortune to summon one of these, they could yabber on and on about bathroom towels and how the weather was so terribly changeable, and what sort of plants were best for indoors. And they would not leave either, even after the séance was over. That was because none of the other dead people would talk to them. So they would float next to you, blathering and blathering without stopping, night and day. In some instances boring dead people literally drove living people insane. In fact, the book said, many psychiatric hospitals are 40 percent full of people who have accidentally summoned a boring ghost.

The dead person Olivia wanted to contact had been anything but boring. She suddenly felt a familiar ache of sadness in her stomach, but she shook it off quickly and returned to reading her book. At the end of the first

chapter, on the very bottom of the page, was a sentence with an asterisk beside it. The sentence said, "Remember, dead people also hold séances to contact living people."

The door to apartment 12K opened and an old woman stepped out. In her arms she cradled a tremendous garbage can. She was very tiny and the can was very large, but she had no trouble carrying it over to the incinerator—which was a little room in the middle of the hallway—opening the door, and dumping the contents down the incinerator chute. On her way back she whistled a little in a melodious fashion. When she spotted Olivia, she stopped. She shook her head sharply.

"This won't do. Up. Up and in. Up and in." She waved her fingers, shooing Olivia away.

Batty old thing, Olivia thought. She looked away and tried her best to ignore the woman. This became difficult as the batty old thing began to walk directly up to her. The woman's legs were bird-skinny. Her panty hose were sagging at her kneecaps and all around her ankles. Then Olivia saw that she wasn't wearing panty hose.

"No debris on the floor." The woman stared down at Olivia. Olivia looked down at the floor. She had not made a mess. The only thing she'd pulled out of her knapsack was the book.

"There is no debris," Olivia replied.

"Get up and go inside. Leave our hallway clean. Flat surfaces. Straight lines."

"I'm locked out, for your information," Olivia said, suddenly realizing that *she* was the debris the woman was talking about.

"Well, then, sit on another floor. Go down to eleven. They have no shame on eleven."

"I won't," Olivia said. "I live on twelve, not eleven. I'm waiting right here." She opened up her book again and pretended to be engrossed in Chapter 2, which was called "How to Break the Ice with Your Ghost." The woman stamped her tiny foot. Her feet were so small that Olivia wondered if she found her shoes in the children's department. The shoes she was wearing were shiny, white patent leather. Olivia had once had shoes like that. Christopher said they made Olivia look like a nurse, so she didn't wear them again.

"Well, aren't you exactly like Princepessa Christina Lilli!" the woman said to Olivia. "Ah, but exactly! Just as stubborn and bad-tempered. Well, I did not suffer it from Her Highness. I will certainly not suffer it from the likes of you. You must come inside. We will have some Cambrian

tea and Poor Richard's tarts. It's exactly what you want."
Olivia had no idea what these were, but she had the feeling that they *were* exactly what she wanted.

"Okay," Olivia said, reluctant to admit defeat, "but I'll only stay for a minute."

"Yes, yes, Miss Full of Pride, whatever you like." The woman rolled her milky eyes at Olivia, and for a second Olivia could see the face of a young woman superimposed on the older, pinched face. It was only for a second and then it vanished. Olivia wondered if that was what it felt like when you saw a ghost.

Olivia snapped her book shut and tucked it back into her knapsack. Then she followed the strange little woman into apartment 12K.

Three

The first thing Olivia thought when she walked into the apartment was that she had stepped out into thin air and was standing in the middle of the sky. It took her a moment to realize why she had this sensation. Everything was made of glass. Everything! Even the floor. You could look down and see the apartment below.

"Close your mouth or someone might yank out your tonsils. Now, go have a seat on the couch and I'll fix us some tea." The couch was not made of glass, thank goodness, but it was made of perfectly see-through plastic, like a giant soap bubble. It squeaked a little when she sat on it, but it turned out to be surprisingly comfortable. Olivia leaned back. She put her feet up on the glass coffee table.

"Do the people downstairs know you can see them?" Olivia asked.

"No. And it's none of their business," the old woman replied.

"How would *you* like it if I spied on *you* all day long?" Olivia said.

"It might teach you a thing or two about proper manners. Take your feet off the coffee table." The old woman shuffled off to the kitchen and Olivia followed. She stared at the floor. Down in 11K, she could see two women sitting at a table, playing cards. One of the women had her coat draped across the back of her chair, and the other was in a plain housedress. Olivia guessed the woman in the housedress was the one who lived in the apartment. She had soft brown hair that was gathered up in an indifferent bun, and a long, pale neck. Her kitchen was a little shabby. A cobweb was strung across the ceiling lamp, and a fat spider clabbered across the web's silky lacing, coming close to Olivia's feet. It startled her, and before she could remember that a sheet of glass lay between them, Olivia stomped her sneaker on the floor. The women in 11K looked up at the ceiling. Their eyes were directly on Olivia's feet, but they did not seem to see Olivia. Then they resumed their card game more intently. Olivia wondered, all of a sudden, if the people who lived above her could see into her apartment too. She thought of all the embarrassing things she did every day and decided she would be more careful about what she did in the future.

"Why isn't your ceiling made of glass too?" Olivia asked.

"Because I don't need to keep an eye on those who are above me."

"Why do you need to keep an eye on the people below you?"

"Because they know the sound of my footsteps, and I do not know the sound of theirs. That makes them formidable enemies," the woman said. Olivia looked down at the mousy woman in the housedress.

"I think you're paranoid," Olivia said.

"The most dangerous people are those who appear most harmless—the scullery maids, the stable boys. That is what Princepessa Christina Lilli always told me."

"Who is Princepessa Christina Lilli?" Olivia asked.

The little woman was filling a glass teakettle from a glass faucet. She put the kettle on the glass stove, set the flame, and marched past Olivia with a glass serving platter full of pastries.

"Who is Princepessa Christina Lilli!?" the little woman repeated Olivia's question. "If the Princepessa had heard you ask that question, she would have given you a smart slap on your cheek."

"And I would have slapped her back," replied Olivia.

"And she would have had you clapped in irons and sent to the tower." The woman put the pastries down. There were five little brown squares that were puffy in the center. "Or she might just as easily have made you into her dearest, best friend. Which fate is worse, I can't tell you. She made me into her dearest, best friend and I served out my sentence for twelve years. Twelve years of temper tantrums and dinners flung at the walls and dresses shredded because the sleeves crinkled up like a walnut shell. She was allergic to walnuts. Made her face swell up something awful.

"Once, when a visiting prince said that my eyes resembled the little amber beach stones he had collected for her, the Princepessa made me wear a black blindfold for an entire year. But she had it made from the finest Babatavian silk, and then she hired a servant to dress me and brush my hair and guide me around the grounds."

Olivia helped herself to one of the pastries. She bit into the tart and found that it was filled with raspberry jam and that it was delicious.

"I wouldn't have stayed if she had treated me like that," she said.

"Don't speak with your mouth full. It's ugly. You *would*

have stayed too. And here's why—because the Princepessa Christina Lilli was simply the most remarkable girl in the world. She was wicked and bold and she made me laugh just a little more than she made me cry. And if you ever meet a single person in your dreary, little life that can half match the Princepessa, you may count yourself lucky." The lady gave a little slap of finality to her leathery kneecap. Then she squinted at the air and rose quickly, shuffling off down the foyer.

She returned a minute later with a huge contraption that rolled along the floor. She pulled it by a long hose with a nozzle shaped like a tuba. She flipped on a switch with a stamp of her little white shoe, and the contraption made a terrific bawling noise, then a dry, gulping sound. She held the hose in the air and waved it all around the room. Just as Olivia began to feel a little light-headed, the old woman shut the contraption off. She pulled up the lid of the machine and took out a clear plastic bag with nothing in it. Then she turned the bag upside down into her huge garbage can. Nothing came out.

"It's shocking how quickly the air gets dirty," she said. "Have another tart. I'll be back in a moment." She left to carry the can of dirty air out to the incinerator room.

While she was gone, Olivia got up and inspected the

place. She kept her arms close to her sides for fear of breaking something. Peeking into the bathroom, she saw a glass toilet bowl and a glass bathtub with carved glass claw feet. Olivia looked down into the bathroom of 11K. Sitting on the bathroom floor was a little boy, about two years old. He was wearing a lumpy diaper and nothing else. In one hand he held a toilet plunger and was pressing the suction cup against the head of a calico cat.

Olivia then went into the old woman's bedroom. Her bed had tall glass posts on every corner, and the covers on the bed were made of gauzy layers of sheer silk—watery pinks and ivories and yellows. She had a glass vanity and a glass dresser, and on top of the dresser was something remarkable: a jet-black, completely opaque box. Olivia walked over to it. She ran her finger across the top of it. It was made of something hard and cold and slick. On the front was a small silver latch and—well, how could she help herself—she pressed on it and the lid snapped open. There, nestled in a rich lining of purple velvet, were some of the most beautiful jewels Olivia had ever seen. They looked like they should be sitting behind glass in a museum. There were glittering diamonds, deep red rubies set in lustrous yellow gold, and pearls as big as a robin's egg. There were rings and bracelets and necklaces all in a tangle. Olivia's mother had had a jewelry box, but Olivia had never been allowed to touch it.

Wouldn't Mom bust a gut if she saw what was in *this* box! Olivia thought. Makes her stuff look like junk.

"Well, Miss Nosey Parker. Miss Sticky Fingers." The old lady had returned and stood at the bedroom door with her arms folded against her flat chest. She didn't really look mad.

"You must be filthy rich," Olivia said.

"I'm neither thing. But I do have my little nest egg. It was given to me by the Princepessa. When the Revolution began, she sewed all her jewels into the hems of her dresses. These baubles were the ones she couldn't find room for. I suppose if I were ever to see her again, she'd ask for it all back. But I don't think I shall ever see her again."

"What happened to her?" Olivia asked. Her fingers were absently stroking a diamond brooch.

"They took her away, those cruel soldiers with the broad black mustaches. Whisked her off, along with her beautiful mama and her father the King. Some people said she died on the long, cold journey to the prison in Refnastova, the capital. But I doubt it. Princepessa Christina Lilli was as tough as a young lioness. I prefer to believe that she kicked and screamed and bit and, in the end, escaped."

The old woman sighed, then plucked Olivia's hand from the box with her cool, papery fingers and shut the lid. "But we shall never know. Life is full of loose ends." The old woman looked very sad now. Olivia considered how lonely she must be. A little batty and definitely exasperating. But lonely, too, in her glass apartment, longing for a friend who was probably dead.

A small movement below caught Olivia's eyes. Down in 11K, the little boy was toddling into a bedroom right below them. He had dropped his toilet plunger and now clutched a blue bottle.

"What is that boy up to now?" the old woman fretted as she watched him plop down on a worn square of rug and begin to fiddle with the top of the bottle. "If his mother would pay as much attention to her child as she does to her blasted cards, he might actually survive to be a rotten, pimply teenager. Last month I had to alert her when he put potting soil in his mouth, and the month before that when the venetian-blind cord nearly strangled him to death."

The blue bottle slipped from the child's grasp and

dropped to the floor. The label on the front of it was clearly visible.

"Hey!" Olivia cried. "That's the stuff my father uses to unclog sinks!"

"Oh my goodness!" The woman ran out of the bedroom into the living room, grabbing a broom on the way. She stood directly over the mother, who was still hunkered over her cards, and began to thump on the floor with her broom. The mother looked up at the ceiling but did not get out of her chair.

"Get up, you stupid woman!" the old lady screamed at the floor. The child's mother began to deal out cards frantically while the other woman rubbed her hands together excitedly.

"You!" The old woman pointed at Olivia. "Go down there. Quickly. Tell that brainless thing that her baby is going to poison itself." She pushed Olivia out the door. "Run, girl!" Olivia ran. She thought of the child twisting off the top of the blue bottle and pouring the nasty liquid into his mouth. Then she ran even faster. She pulled open the door to the stairwell and ran as fast as she could, taking the stairs three at a time.

Four

By the time Olivia reached apartment 11K and began to bang on the door, her heart was racing in her chest. It seemed to take forever for anyone to answer. She could hear a chair scraping back against the floor, then the slow sluff-sluff of slippers. Olivia pounded on the door again and rang the bell five times in a row for emphasis.

"Coming," came the thin voice. Just when Olivia thought her heart was going to explode, the door opened. Olivia didn't even bother to speak. There was no time. She pushed past the woman, nearly throwing her down, and ran to the back room. The apartment had the same layout as the old woman's, so she easily found the child's bedroom. The little boy had managed to take off the bottle's cap and was now sitting with his tongue extended, tipping the bottle toward his mouth. Olivia swooped down on him, knocking the bottle out of his hands. She wound up with the child directly beneath her while he was screaming his lungs out, but the blue bottle was lying a few feet away, the thick liquid trickling out onto the floor.

"What kind of mother are you anyway!?" Olivia snapped angrily at the woman, who was now standing at the bedroom door, looking very confused.

"Who are you?" the woman asked. Her eyes were wide. She suddenly noticed her crying child and swept him up into her arms.

"Your kid was walking around with poison in his hands," Olivia said angrily, pointing at the blue bottle leaking fluid onto the carpet, "and you're busy with your dumb cards!"

"How did you know Patrick was going to drink that?" the woman asked, looking from Olivia to the bottle.

"I saw it," Olivia snapped back.

"Mmm, you saw it . . . you saw it." The woman nodded knowingly. She didn't appear the least upset about her child, who was already wriggling out of her arms. On the contrary, she seemed delighted as she stared at Olivia with her average-colored eyes. In fact the woman was so average in every way—average height, average-sized nose, average lips—that Olivia considered she might need to meet her a dozen times or more before she could pick her out in a crowd.

"We're exactly alike, you and I," the woman said. Considering what Olivia had just been thinking, she found this a little insulting. Olivia believed herself anything but average. Her brother, Christopher, always said that Olivia was the most first-rate kid on the planet, and he dared his friends to name someone more first-rate than his sister. They never did—they knew better than to argue with Christopher on the subject of his sister.

"I don't think we're at all alike," Olivia said.

"We're both clairvoyant. We both have the gift of seeing the future. But you must be better at it than I am. I've never *seen* an event before it happened. I only hear things. It started two months ago. It was Patrick's birthday and I was waiting all day for a card from my husband to come in the mail—my husband's in the navy, so he's always on some ship or other. I waited in the lobby so I could see when the mailman came in, and when he did, I practically tore apart his sack of mail, looking for the card. There was nothing there. Not a thing.

"Well, I went back upstairs and cried so hard that I gave myself a headache. I lay down on the couch with a cold washcloth over my eyes. It was then that I heard the rapping above me. Tap, tap, tap. I tried to ignore it but it grew louder . . . thump, thump, thump. Then bang, bang, bang! I got up to see what it was, and the moment I stood, the sound began to travel above my head, down the hallway. I followed it . . . bang, bang, bang! It led me right into Patrick's bedroom, where I found him turning blue with the cord of the venetian blind wrapped around his neck. Since then it has happened again and again. First I hear the tapping, then I find that something terrible is about to happen and I prevent it just in time.

"Now my husband seems to have forgotten about us altogether. He stopped writing. He hasn't sent us any money for rent. I've sold off almost everything we had so we could pay last month's bills. I just started to give tarot card readings, and that helps. I have a few regular customers. Thank heavens for that! Otherwise, there's no telling what would have happened to Patrick and me. Oh, I almost forgot—I still have a customer in the living room. What's your name?"

"Olivia."

"My name is Alice. Oh, look! Patrick adores you already." It was true. The boy was making little hops up toward Olivia with his hands outstretched. She wasn't nuts about small kids in general, but having saved Patrick's life, she felt sort of fond of the troublemaker. She picked him up and he wrapped his arms around her neck. His head smelled nice—like warm biscuits.

Olivia followed Alice into the kitchen, where the other woman still sat at the table, looking terrified. Her hand was clutching at her heart, her eyes raised toward the ceiling. Olivia noticed that the apartment had a completely normal ceiling. You couldn't see through it at all.

"The spirit must have left," the woman at the table whispered in a horrified rasp. "The tapping has stopped." Alice listened for a moment, then nodded her head.

"He's gone," Alice said.

"Oh, you are gifted, Alice," the woman said, standing up and grabbing her coat off the back of the chair. "To conjure spirits like that!" Olivia was just about to tell them that the tapping was only the old lady upstairs, but then she saw the woman at the table reach into her purse and pull out a twenty-dollar bill and hand it to Alice.

"I feel so much better, Alice," the woman said. "So relieved. And the cards never lie, do they?"

"No, ma'am, they never do," said Alice. It was then that Olivia really took a good look at the cards. They were not normal playing cards. They were larger and each one had an elaborate picture on it. The box they came out of had Tarot

Cards printed on it. Olivia knew about tarot cards. Supposedly you could tell people's fortunes with them. A girl at school had once brought in a deck of tarot cards and read Olivia's fortune in the cafeteria in exchange for a miniature box of Milk Duds. The girl wore her hair in a single, thick braid, and she had a lot of hair on her arms. She told Olivia that she would have to go on a dangerous journey. And depending on whether or not she came out of it alive, she would marry a man with a mustache and have two kids. All of which Olivia might have believed had the girl not added, popping a Milk Dud between her lips, "You had a fight with your mother this week. It was about clothes. Don't worry, she'll come around." That was when Olivia knew the tarot cards were fake. Her mother had been gone for a year and a half.

Oh well, Olivia thought, feeling Patrick's hands twisting in her hair. Alice might be a faker, but at least it helps them to buy food and pay the rent. At least she doesn't do it for a few lousy Milk Duds.

The woman made another appointment with Alice for next week, then left.

"Well," Olivia said, putting Patrick down, "I guess I'll be going too."

"Olivia," Alice said, grabbing her elbow, "it was no accident that we met today, today of all days."

"Oh, I'm sure we would have met sooner or later," Olivia said. "My father is the super." Alice was so excitable and she looked so worn-out to begin with that Olivia tried to be as calm as possible.

"But today, this evening, at seven o'clock, Madame Brenda is coming!" Alice's eyes blinked rapidly as she looked toward Olivia for a reaction.

"Who's Madame Brenda?" Olivia asked. But still, something about that name sounded familiar.

"Madame Brenda is the most renowned medium alive. She's very, very old . . . some say she may be past a hundred. She's held thousands of séances, and she hardly ever fails to contact a spirit. And she's coming to see *me!*"

"Why?"

"She's looking for someone to take over the mediumship business for her. But the person has to be very gifted. She's been traveling all over the world searching for her protégé, but hasn't found her yet." Right then Olivia remembered who Madame Brenda was. She opened up her knapsack and pulled out her book on séances. Sure enough, the author of the book was Madame Brenda.

"I don't really have any hope that she'll pick me," Alice continued. "I'm very average as far as psychics go. But you, Olivia! Well, Madame Brenda might choose you!"

"I doubt it," Olivia said. Still, if Madame Brenda *could* contact any ghost, then maybe she could contact Olivia's ghost! "Maybe I'll come anyway," Olivia added. "Seven o'clock, you said?"

"Seven sharp. She's very strict, I hear." Patrick was clinging to Olivia's leg, so she picked him up one last time and planted a kiss on his dirty face. She found that she felt happy—a feeling she had not experienced for nearly a year. It was a strange, weightless sensation. She hoped it lasted.

Five

Olivia returned to the stairwell to walk back up to the twelfth floor. She'd wait for her father in the hallway, no matter what that odd little lady said. But once inside the stairwell Olivia was confronted by the two girls who had been in the elevator with her. They were sitting on the steps, passing a cigarette between them and laughing. When Olivia opened the door, they quickly snubbed it out against the wall and flicked it behind them. But when they saw that it was only Olivia, they both looked peeved to have wasted the cigarette. And Olivia suddenly remembered her pant cuffs.

"Ever hear of knocking?" the glamorous one asked Olivia.

"Ever hear of public property?" Olivia replied.

The other girl, the grinning one, liked Olivia's answer. "Snap!" the grinning girl said approvingly to Olivia.

"Sting!" She guffawed very stupidly and poked one of her pointy fingers into the glamorous girl's ribs. "She got you, Renee! She got you good!"

"Shut up, darling Gretchen," Renee said. "What apartment do you live in anyway?" she asked Olivia.

"Twelve C," Olivia said.

"Oh, so your father is the new janitor?" Renee said.

"He's the superintendent."

"Darling, you can call a hamburger 'filet mignon' but the fact remains. Anyway . . . my friend Gretchen here believes that she knows you." Olivia turned to Gretchen, whose grinning suddenly stopped. "Gretchen says she saw you in the waiting room of the school's counseling services. That means you are either stealing things or starving yourself. Or you're having mental problems. Gretchen steals things." Gretchen's face had turned a little pink and she was biting at her upper lip. "So," Renee said, "what do you do?"

"Nothing," Olivia muttered.

"Then you must be having mental problems. Are you a head case?"

"No," said Olivia.

"Well, I suppose if you *were* a head case, you wouldn't know it." Renee shrugged and took out a little bag from her back pocket. It was full of sunflower seeds. She popped one open with her front teeth, then swallowed the tiny gray seed.

"Do you have any brothers?" Renee asked.

"Just one," Olivia replied.

"How old?"

"Twenty," Olivia said.

"Well," the glamorous girl said impatiently, "is he cute or what?"

Olivia looked at Renee. She was really a very pretty girl, Olivia thought. She wondered what Christopher would think of her. Before he went to college, he used to bring home his girlfriends. They were all completely different. Some were tall and some were squat, some were plain and some were beautiful; some wore perfume that smelled like tea roses and others dyed their own clothes. But Christopher said they all had "the eye." And "the eye" was the only thing that mattered. Olivia looked in the glamorous girl's eyes. They were a liquidy deep brown. Her lashes were thick and shiny. They were beautiful eyes. But they seemed to be sifting through the world for things that she wanted. Olivia decided that, although Renee was glamorous, she definitely did not have "the eye."

"You're not his type."

"Of course I'm his type," Renee cried. "I'm *everybody's*

type." Renee's lips had grown very small and compressed. She snorted like an angry horse. Gretchen was grinning again. "Where is he? Let him meet me."

"He's at college," Olivia said.

"I don't believe you. Let's go to your apartment."

"I'm locked out of my apartment," Olivia said.

Renee squinted at her. She obviously thought Olivia was lying. "I know where your father is. You can get the key from him," she said.

"Where is he!?" Olivia asked.

"If I tell you, will you introduce me to your brother?"

"Fine, yes. Where's my father?"

"He's down at Sidi's apartment," said Renee. "He's fixing the heat down there." Then Renee and Gretchen exchanged glances. Gretchen's grin was wider than ever, and Renee popped a sunflower seed into her mouth to hide her own smile. She neglected to spit out the hull and ate the seed whole, then choked a little.

"Fine," said Olivia. "Where is Sidi's apartment?"

"I'll take you!" Gretchen cried out and jumped to her feet.

"I thought you weren't supposed to go to Sidi's apartment anymore, Gretchen," Renee said slyly. "I thought you made some sort of idiotic promise to your parents."

"I'll go for just a minute," Gretchen said. Her dullish eyes had suddenly grown bright, and she was blinking rapidly.

"Oh, well," Renee said, standing up. "I guess I'll go too." And all three of them started down the steps. Olivia's afternoon had been so peculiar that she forgot all about giving her father the Silent Treatment. Now she couldn't wait to find him and to watch his soft, craggy features crumple up in happiness when he saw her. To go home. To curl up on the living room couch with a slice of toast and raspberry jam and the ancient grandfather clock ticking out its tireless pulse.

When they got to the seventh floor, Renee opened the stairwell door and they all walked down the hallway. Renee's steps were a little more hesitant now. When they reached the door, Renee gave Olivia's shoulder a little shove: "Go on. It's *your* father. Ring the bell."

Six

There was no buzzer for the apartment. But a cunning little hole had been drilled through the metal door, and coming out of the hole was a length of red ribbon with a brass ring on the end of it. Tentatively, Olivia slipped her finger through the ring and gave it a yank. A series of chimes rang. The door opened almost immediately, as if swept in by a sudden gust of wind. Hot wind. Well, Renee hadn't lied. There was something terribly wrong with the heat, that much was clear.

A tiny man in a smoking jacket stood at the door. He cut a neat, elegant figure with his small manicured fingernails and a crisply clipped beard that was absolutely white. Olivia had seen this same man once or twice before, in the elevator carrying a large bouquet of flowers. He had always struck Olivia as rather adorable.

"May I help you?" He smiled sweetly at the girls.

"I'm looking for my father," Olivia said. "George Kidney?"

"Has he been missing a long time?" the little man asked. "Because we don't keep people longer than six or seven days. Not that we wouldn't *like* to. But there's the problem of space . . . and of course the families begin to worry, tut tut tut. But come in and have a look around." The little man opened the door wider and Olivia stepped in. Gretchen and Renee followed her.

It was like walking into a rain forest. All around, the foliage was so thick that she could not make out where the walls started, or if there were any walls at all. Huge heart-shaped leaves drooped down, tickling the top of Olivia's head, while a dense undergrowth of ferns and giant purple, pink, and white orchids brushed against her jeans. Overhead a spiraling tangle of vines crawled across the ceiling. The girls followed the little man as he pushed through the vegetation. The air was so hot that it felt tropical, quivering in waves. It gave Olivia the sensation of being smothered by a damp washcloth.

"The heat is terrible in here," Olivia said, gasping.

"Isn't it though!?" the little man agreed. "Poor Sidi is in a state!"

"You're not Sidi?" Olivia asked.

"Me?" The little man touched both hands to his chest and giggled. Behind her, Gretchen and Renee laughed too, but rather nervously. Then the man turned and continued on. Olivia felt a rush of air beside her ear and a white cockatiel flew by, its soft wings touching her face, then disappeared into the green depths. Never in her life had she lived in such a strange apartment building!

Finally the foliage opened out onto a large, shady parlor. Olivia had expected to see many people, but the only person in the room was a slender woman wrapped in a multicolored shawl and shivering in a wicker chair. She had a mass of kinky silver hair that she'd coiled on top of her head.

"Better, Sidi?" the little man asked a little shyly.

"No," Sidi said angrily. "What's taking the super so long?"

"He's fixing it," the little man assured her.

"Then my father's here?" Olivia asked.

"Well, he's not fixing it fast enough," Sidi continued petulantly. "I'm still freezing. And what are *those* two doing here anyway? I thought I told you girls not to come back."

"Please, Sidi," Renee said in the sweetest voice she could muster. "We're not empty-handed this time."

"Your hands look empty to me," Sidi snorted. She unbound her hair and let it unravel to a thick, silver mantle that reached the base of her spine. Her fingers tickled a conch shell that was sitting on top of a little table beside her chair. Gretchen and Renee both sucked in their breath.

"I'm just going to talk to my father for a minute," Olivia said.

"Don't disturb him!" cried Sidi. Her face had the look of faceted marble, finely cut but rather inhuman. "My orchids are wilting from the cold, and my poor lizards will catch their death."

It was then that Olivia realized that Sidi's shawl was not really a shawl. It was, in fact, hundreds of lizards. They were all different colors—purple, yellow, green, orange. They had climbed on top of Sidi and shrouded her with their rubbery bodies. One of them clambered up on Olivia's sneaker. She screamed and kicked it off.

"Hey, Buster!" the lizard cried out as it flew through the air. At least that's what it sounded like.

The heat was making Olivia woozy. Her eyes felt swollen and watery. A trickle of sweat leaked down her temple.

"But how can my father work in this heat?" Olivia groaned. She knew he had enough trouble fixing things under the best conditions.

"Your father is in the back room, which we keep rather cool," the little man said. "He's perfectly comfortable, I assure you."

Olivia closed her eyes and her head dipped toward her chest.

"Ah, but you're not well," the little man said.

"The heat—," Olivia mumbled.

"Sit down, my dear." He took her elbow in his manicured fingers.

"My father. I have to see . . ."

"Come," he urged her with a gentle pressure at her elbow. "Have a seat in our parlor. Perhaps Sidi will play for you. Wouldn't that be lovely?"

Seven

The little gentleman led Olivia to a sofa, a shapeless thing that felt like sitting on a very fat woman. As Olivia's body pressed into the cushion, the stuffing rolled up around her like billows of flesh. She felt cradled in a very pleasant way.

"Please, Sidi," Renee was cajoling. "Play for us. Just for a few minutes!"

"Why should I?" Sidi replied. She rubbed her hands together and shivered lightly. "You have no money. No jewelry. You have nothing that I want."

"*She's* got stuff." Renee nodded toward Olivia. "She's got a whole knapsack full of stuff."

"Fetch me her knapsack, Johansson," Sidi ordered the little gentleman.

"Certainly." Johansson smiled down at Olivia and, with a most courteous bow, removed the knapsack from Olivia's shoulder. She moved to grab it back, but her body was so weak from the heat that she could not move fast enough.

"Open it," Sidi ordered.

Johansson unzipped the knapsack. He pushed his hand around inside, pulled out the old door chain, and held it up for Sidi's inspection. She touched it briefly with her fingertips, then waved it away.

"What else?" she said in a bored voice. Johansson reached in the knapsack again and pulled out a book.

"No," Olivia protested. Her voice sounded as if she were submerged underwater. Her breath joined the waves of heat in the air.

"A nice book," Johansson said. "A handsome book. A book on . . ." He checked the cover. "Séances."

"Mmmm," Sidi considered, then reached for the book.

"*My* book," Olivia said, but when her words hit the air, they withered to an infant's gurgle. Sidi turned Madame Brenda's book on séances over in her large, fine hands. She opened it and flipped through the pages.

"All right then. I'll take this," Sidi said, and she tossed it on the floor beside her. Then she picked up a conch shell and began to blow into it. To say that it was "music" was not strictly true. The sound that Sidi made with her conch shell was like the ocean—it rose and fell in mysterious patterns, like waves, and it beckoned you to come closer, come closer. The heat didn't seem to bother Olivia so much while the music was playing. In the corner, Gretchen and Renee were reclining on pillows. They were so still that they looked like department-store mannequins. Their mouths were hanging open.

It is worth it, Olivia thought dreamily. I would have given her *all* of Christopher's books to hear her play.

"You *will* give her all his books," Gretchen muttered. Apparently Olivia had spoken her thoughts out loud. "And all your allowance. And when you have no more allowance money, you'll start stealing things for Sidi. But it's sooo worth it. Even if they send you to the school shrink. It's all worth it."

"Shut up," Renee murmured. She was wearing the same spooky grin as Gretchen now.

Olivia sank back into the couch. She could no longer feel the surface of her skin. Her body was dissolving, liquefying like butter in a saucepan. She didn't mind at all. In fact, it was a relief. She felt quite comfortable. All worries and sadness left her. Unburdened, her mind was as light as a soap bubble. It rose up to the ceiling and hovered there.

The white cockatiel flew by, fixing a dark, curious eye

on Olivia's mind as it passed. From above Olivia could look down at the tops of everyone's head, even her own. She noticed that the part in her hair was very straight and marveled that she had ever cared enough to comb it so carefully. Her body looked so small and feeble, slumped on the couch. How had she navigated through life in such a fragile container? She looked like a toy doll with movable limbs.

Then she remembered something. Her mother used to collect dolls. She had purchased them from the Home Shopping Channel on television and put them all in a massive curio cabinet in the dining room. She had posed them so that they each seemed to be intensely interested in one another; the Victorian bride doll looked riveted by the boy in a baseball cap eating a bowl of peas. The little geisha doll was caught in midbow to the baby in a christening gown. None of them looked out through the thin glass. None of them appeared to notice their predicament.

One day Olivia's mother bought two dolls, a brother and sister doll that were a matching set. They cost her a great deal of money, and they were very well crafted, with faces that were eerily human. But even more eerie was the fact that they looked exactly like Olivia and Christopher.

Their mother was thrilled at the resemblance. Whenever guests came over, she always pointed out the dolls proudly, and some guests wondered, in the car ride home, if Mrs. Kidney were prouder of the dolls than of the real children.

Then, one day, the brother and sister dolls were missing from the curio cabinet. Olivia's mother shrieked and then interrogated everyone in the house. When that came to nothing, she tore the house apart. When *that* came to nothing, she went into her bedroom and cried. No one knew what to do. No one went to comfort her, not even Mr. Kidney. They knew better than to disturb her when she was in a state. No one made a move until she had cried herself to sleep.

Later that night Olivia went to Christopher's room. Christopher was lying on his bed, his long blond arms crossed behind his head. He looked relaxed, happy. Olivia frowned.

"You made Mom cry," she said.

"I didn't mean to," he said calmly. Then he shifted his eyes to look at her. "How did you know it was me who took the dolls?" he asked.

"I just knew. Where did you put them?"

"In a safe place," he said.

"But why did you do it?" Olivia asked. Christopher sat up and put his bare feet on top of hers. Sometimes he told her things and sometimes he didn't.

"Mom associated them too much with us," he said. "That made them effigies."

"What are effigies?"

"They are things that can be used as a substitute for a real person. People can do things to an effigy and it will affect the real person."

"Like voodoo dolls?" Olivia asked. In Christopher's bedroom was a bookcase squeezed tight with all types of books. But a lot of them were mystical books—about spirits and deities from other religions and about magic. She had found a book on voodoo in his bookshelf and had read it cover to cover.

"Yeah, something like voodoo dolls," Christopher said.

"But Mom wouldn't stick pins in those dolls or anything," Olivia protested.

"No. But she might accidentally drop one on its head. Or decide to separate the two of them because the brother doll looks better with the giant redheaded clown doll. Or their paint might crack or there could be a fire. It could be anything. But don't worry, kiddo. I've taken care of it. We'll be fine."

But as it turned out, they had *not* been fine. Things had gone very, very wrong, and Olivia now wondered if someone had found those hidden dolls after all. She looked down at her own doll-like body on the couch.

"No!" she cried out. But the word pawed around inside her brain and could not seem to find its way out through her lips. She launched herself downward toward her body. She felt her mind slam violently back into her skull. It was painful, like a small explosion in her head. Her vision was blurry and she could hear only muffled sounds. Struggling, her muscles contracted and twitched while the fleshy cushion clenched up around her limbs like a giant blood-pressure gauge, sucking her back within its clutches. Gathering up all her strength, she hurled herself off the couch. Her breath was sucked out of her lungs and her knees buckled when her feet hit the floor. But she steadied herself and staggered directly up to Sidi. Sidi stopped playing and stared at Olivia.

"That—is—my—book." Olivia said the words with difficulty but firmness. She bent down and snatched the book up. The look on Sidi's face was one of sheer astonishment. She looked as though she had never, in her entire life, had a thing taken away from her. Olivia took back her knapsack too, put the book inside it, and zipped it up tight. For a moment everyone in the room stiffened in dread.

"Get that book, Johansson," Sidi snarled. The little gentleman bit his thumb for a moment. Olivia readied herself for a struggle.

Johansson approached her. He tilted his head and smiled.

"If you come with me out to the terrace, miss, I will tell you a story. Perhaps you will change your mind about giving Sidi what she desires." Johansson opened the terrace door. A burst of fresh, cool air rushed in. It felt delicious against Olivia's heated skin.

"I won't change my mind," she said. Still, she needed to get out of the smothering heat. Clutching her knapsack securely against her chest, she said, "But while I wait for my father, I'll listen to your story." Then she followed Johansson out to the terrace.

Eight

After clearing his throat once or twice, Johansson began: "There once was a ship that used to sail in the Mediterranean, around the Hydrocophegene Islands. The ship was built in the most peculiar way . . . it was turned up on its side so that it looked exactly like it had capsized and was in the process of sinking into the ocean. The sight of the sinking ship never failed to stop other ships in their course. The other ships would throw down their life preservers for the passengers, who they assumed must be drowning in the violent, roiling water. And sure enough, they would heave up a dozen or more wet sailors whom they had saved from certain death. But these were no ordinary sailors. They were bandits. And no ordinary bandits either. They were some of the most dangerous, deranged bandits that had ever gathered for a single purpose. Their leader was Master Clive, a six-foot eight-inch butcher of a man who had an aversion to dirtying his hands, so he always wore black rubber gloves to keep the blood off them.

"Once on board the ship that had 'saved' them, the bandits would, at sword-point, force all the ship's crew into burlap sacks, bind them tightly, and drop them one by one into the ocean. Then they would ransack the ship for valuables and amuse themselves with the passengers, if there were any, by various forms of torture. Master Clive loved to tie a rope around passengers' ankles and dangle them in shark-infested water. Sometimes the bandits would have the ship's cook prepare a tremendous feast for themselves and order the passengers to perform for them. It was a talent show of sorts where the passengers would nervously sing or dance or tell jokes. But for the most part the passengers were a wealthy, spoiled lot. If they had ever wanted entertainment, they simply purchased it, and consequently they had never needed to learn how to entertain themselves. So they were, generally, very untalented. It was quite a sight to see Mrs. Periwinkle-Hudson, the grand heiress of the Periwinkle Pickle fortune, leap around in a tutu made of wilted cabbage heads, or Senator Breakwater of Tennessee make fart noises with his armpits. The talent contest had only one winner, whose prize was to be set adrift in a lifeboat with a flask of water and a day's worth of food. The losers were tossed overboard.

"Well, one day the bandits spotted a ship called the SS *Rosenquist*. The ship was a gigantic luxury liner, the size of three football fields from bow to stern. Yet the ship was almost entirely empty. On board was the ship's captain, the steward, the ship's cook, and the cook's young daughter. Other than that, there was only one single passenger. The passenger had chartered the ship with the condition that he or she would be the only passenger aboard. It made the captain a little suspicious—for he had never seen the passenger in person and wondered if it was a criminal—but a thick envelope of cash put his mind at ease.

"So far none of the ship's little crew had seen their mysterious passenger. The passenger stayed in his or her cabin. It was the smallest cabin on the ship. The steward brought all the passenger's meals to the cabin, knocked twice, and left the tray outside the cabin door. Then the passenger put the dirty plates back outside the door, and occasionally a full can of trash or soiled sheets, and the steward took them away.

"In the evenings, under the stars, the crew would argue over their passenger's identity.

" 'I think she's a movie star,' claimed the cook. 'You can tell because she eats very little and movie stars are always dieting.' The others considered this for a few minutes, listening to the waves as they splashed against the side of the ship.

" 'No,' the steward said. 'I believe you're wrong. Movie stars like to look at themselves in the mirror. And our passenger chose the smallest cabin, which has only the tiniest morsel of a mirror hanging above the bathroom sink. No, definitely not a movie star! I think our passenger is a distinguished mathematician working on an important theorem.'

" 'What do you think, Delilah?' the captain asked the cook's daughter. Delilah was only five years old and very small for her age, but she was exceedingly wise. She raised her eyes to the sky and watched as a plane groaned overhead. She wondered if it was Sidi, the famous teenage pilot who was making her much-publicized trip around the world in her twin-engine plane. Delilah had photos of Sidi plastered all around her cabin and even had an autographed eight-by-ten glossy photo of the young pilot on which was scribbled, 'To Delilah . . . maybe one day our paths will cross. Until then, keep your eye on the sky!' Delilah waved at the plane as it disappeared into black clouds.

" 'I think,' said Delilah, 'that if we found out who our

passenger was tonight, we would have nothing to argue about tomorrow. And then our trip would be very dull.'

"But even if they had found out who their passenger was that night, their trip would not have been dull. Because the very next day the SS *Rosenquist* came upon a capsized ship. The little crew hurried to rescue the 'drowning' bandits. They tossed down life preservers and heaved them all up one at a time. Even little Delilah helped. The last one they pulled on board was Master Clive, and they had to labor very hard indeed to haul his bulk up the side of the ship and onto the promenade.

" 'Thank you, my friends!' Master Clive said as he wrung the ocean out of his shirt. He was wearing his black rubber gloves. 'You are a brave and admirable little crew. It will be a great privilege to murder you.' At that, all the bandits whipped out their swords and promptly forced the captain and the steward into burlap sacks, tied them tightly, and tossed them into the water. They kept the cook alive to prepare their customary feast, but Master Clive swept Delilah up by the collar of her shirt and moved to hurl her overboard.

" 'But sir!' Delilah's father cried. 'My daughter is the only one who can prepare a proper onion soufflé. It is the ship's specialty!' Master Clive hesitated for a moment while

Delilah dangled over the edge of the ship. Then, with a sweep of his tremendous arm, he planted Delilah back on the ship's deck and patted her head fondly with his gloved hand.

" 'If your daddy is lying, my sweet, I will slice off all your fingers and toes and feed them to the gulls.'

"The cook and his daughter went to work while the bandits, deciding to save their looting and pillaging until after their meal, drank up the ship's reserves of wine. The onion soufflé proved to be as featherlight as Master Clive could wish for, and by the end of the meal they were all well soused and shouting for a talent show. They beckoned the cook, told him the rules of their talent show, and ordered him to gather up the guests.

" 'Your daughter must be in the show too,' said Master Clive. 'She has well-made little feet and I should like to see her dance.' Now the cook began to panic. He knew that only one other passenger was aboard, and that the passenger, whether a movie star or a brilliant mathematician, would certainly outshine his poor little Delilah. He knew Delilah could not dance. She would lose the talent show and be tossed into the ocean.

" 'There are no other passengers aboard this ship,' the cook lied.

" 'Nonsense,' said Master Clive.

" 'Haven't you noticed how silent it is, sir? We have deposited all our passengers in Mauritius. There is not another soul on board except myself and my child.'

" 'Search the cabins!' Master Clive roared, and his men stood up, weaving around from all the wine, and tottered out to search the cabins. They scattered about the ship, yanking open cabin doors with great gusto at first. But the effects of the wine got the better of them, and they gave up before they had come upon the smallest cabin with the mysterious passenger.

" 'It's a regular ghost ship!' they told Master Clive on their return. 'There t'ain't a body to be found.' This put Master Clive in a foul temper. With no passengers there would be no robbery, no torture, no murder. He hated that. His eyes narrowed to savage slits. He had taken off his black rubber gloves to eat, but now he put them back on again. His eyes turned to Delilah.

" 'We will have our talent show in any case. You . . . girl! Go to the middle of the room and dance!'

" 'I will not,' Delilah said. The cook buried his head in his hands, assured now of his child's doom.

" 'Then I will kill your father,' Master Clive said.

" 'You will kill him anyway,' said Delilah. 'And since I

look very foolish when I dance, I will not dance. But I am willing to whistle a little.'

" 'Whistle? That's very ordinary. Why don't you balance this cup and saucer on your head while you whistle?'

" 'No,' Delilah said. Master Clive frowned, then grimaced.

" 'Okay,' Master Clive said. 'Whistle, then. But I warn you . . . whistling is one of those things that usually irritates me. Imagine how unpleasant I can be when I am irritated.'

"Delilah walked to the center of the room. She pushed her hair behind her ears and cleared her throat. Her father had dropped to the floor by now—his nerves simply could not take any more, and he had fainted. Delilah licked her lips, then took in a single, long breath. She puckered up and raised her chin.

"The noise she produced cannot be described in words. Suffice it to say, after five minutes Master Clive's hard, cruel brain began to think about his mother and the scent of lilies of the valley and of how brief and sad was a man's life. He began to cry. When the other bandits stared, he stabbed one of them in the hand with a fork. Before long the other men succumbed to similar sentimental thoughts, and they put their heads down on the table and wept.

"Then Delilah stopped. The men looked up at her,

teary-eyed, like small children. She stared back at them. Her face grew stern. Her little chest billowed out while she took in a great gulp of air and began to whistle again.

"Her whistling had changed now. It was harsh and piercing. At first, the sound was merely disturbing to the bandits. They could not understand why that sweet symphony had changed. They plugged their ears with bits of bread. But the sound fought its way past the bread plugs and into the bandits' ear canals. Once the sound was inside their heads, the bandits realized that it was the collective screams of every man, woman, and child they had ever killed. It was the most dreadful, ghastly sound. It drove them quite mad. They slapped at their heads to drive out the sound; they fell to the ground and slammed their heads against the floor. Finally one of them took out his long sword and cut off his own head. The others, seeing the logic of this, took up their long swords and did the same until every bandit was headless, as well as dead. Except Master Clive. His constitution was stronger than any of his men, and although he was clutching his head in agony, he did not succumb to the long sword solution. Instead, dragging his body across the floor, he managed to grab Delilah by her shoe. He tried to pull her down and strangle the whistle from her lips, but Delilah was too nimble. Yanking her foot up, she slipped out of her shoe and ran. Her father, who had recovered from his faint, caught her up in his arms and the two of them escaped from the dining hall, with Master Clive hard on their heels.

" 'I will pull out both your hearts and pickle them in brine!' Master Clive's voice was close behind them, so close that they could smell the onion soufflé on his breath. A flash of black rubber grazed the cook's throat just as he turned into the pantry and bolted the door right in Master Clive's face. From one of the shelves the cook pulled down a large wooden salad bowl. Then he fumbled through the drawers and found two long wooden spoons. By this time Master Clive was banging on the door so hard that the door's hinges were beginning to tear away from the frame.

"Quickly the cook put Delilah in the salad bowl and handed her the two wooden spoons. Then he placed the bowl in a net bag that was used to hold garlic cloves and, with great care, he lowered the bowl out the porthole and onto the rolling ocean waves.

" 'Paddle with the spoons, Delilah!' he called down to her. Delilah looked up at her father. She knew she would never see him again. Then a surging wave whisked the salad bowl up on its crest and pulled her out, away from the SS *Rosenquist*, into the cold, blank ocean.

Nine

⁶⁶As Delilah paddled away, she watched the SS *Rosenquist* grow smaller and smaller until it became a black pea in the horizon, and then, phhttt!—it was gone. All that was left was ocean, stretching out as far as Delilah could see in every direction. Through the whole night and into the next day, Delilah floated in her salad bowl, paddling faster when she spotted shark fins cutting through the water or when she thought she saw a black spot of land in the distance (which always turned out to be a nasty trick of shadows). She wondered about her dear father, allowing herself exactly 1.5 percent hope that he was still alive. She also wondered about the mysterious passenger. Would Master Clive discover the passenger in the end? Perhaps the passenger had jumped overboard, and Delilah would meet him or her, floating in a life preserver. Then at least Delilah would have company. For what frightened Delilah most—

more than sharks or Master Clive or even death itself—was being alone.

"As the sun rose, the air grew very hot. Delilah was terribly thirsty, but the ocean was full of salt and could not quench her thirst. Sweat poured down her face and she had to keep dousing her head with handfuls of water to keep from passing out. She had never in her life felt such powerful heat. It seemed to rise up from the core of the earth rather than from the sun overhead. She wilted in her salad bowl just like a dried-out piece of lettuce. She no longer had the energy to paddle.

"She must have fallen asleep, because the next thing she knew, she was tossed out of the bowl rather violently. She was on land.

"Standing up, wobbly from the heat and from being scrunched in the salad bowl, she looked around. She appeared to have landed on some kind of island. Flanking the shore was a short beach, a few yards of soft, pale sand. The sand was very hot, so she walked into the shade of a thick forest that seemed to make up the rest of the island. It was a forest of the tropical variety where everything grew too large, even the insects. The birds were the size of monkeys and the chattering monkeys were the size of bear cubs and the snakes had jaws that could open up and swallow Delilah whole. She took great care to avoid the snakes.

"She made the island her home and lived there peacefully. She grew quite used to the intense heat and, in fact, came to prefer it. She found plenty of fruit to eat from the trees. She learned to catch fish with her bare hands and liked to eat them raw, biting their heads off with her teeth. The snakes gave her no more trouble after she learned how to strangle them. All in all, life was going rather well for Delilah. Except that she was miserable. Her loneliness was like a scream without any sound. In fact, she had bad dreams at night in which she would scream and scream, but no sound would come out of her mouth. And when she woke up, she *was* screaming, but no one was there to hear or comfort her, so it was very like making no sound at all.

"Then one day, she picked up a conch shell that had been washed up on shore and began to blow into it. The sound it produced was clear and sweet, and Delilah amused herself for many hours by whistling to the ocean. It seemed to her—perhaps because she was so desperately lonely—that the ocean was listening. The waves came to the shore faster and faster, like crowds of people rushing toward a spectacle. The wind picked up and blew hard, whipping her hair about her head, and the waves rose higher and higher.

"In the distance she saw one particularly long, low, dark wave coming slowly toward the island. It approached far more slowly than the other waves. It wobbled to the right and to the left, and seemed to be a rather feeble kind of wave, but still it persisted in its awkward approach. After a few minutes Delilah could make out that it was not a wave at all, but a cluster of men swimming toward the island. She was so shocked that she let the conch shell fall from her lips.

"But the moment she did, the men stopped swimming and began to flounder about in the water, screaming for help. She put the shell back to her lips and blew into it again. The men stopped shouting and once more began to swim methodically toward the island. And so she played on until all twelve of the men were safely on shore. After they had caught their breaths and wrung out their mustaches, the sailors told Delilah they had been working aboard a freighter traveling through the Hydrocophegene Islands. When they had heard the beautiful music, they felt the irresistible desire to jump ship and swim toward it with all their might.

"Delilah was thrilled for the company. Right away she organized games of charades and Name That Sea Anemone. She fixed her visitors the best foods the island had to offer and showed them how to strangle the snakes. But happy as Delilah was to have them on her island, the men themselves were not happy at all. 'It is *so* hot!' they complained. 'The heat could drive a person mad! And there is nothing to eat but bananas and fluke.'

" 'And grubs,' Delilah reminded them. 'And crawlers. Which are very succulent when they're in season.' But the men would not be consoled. The only thing that silenced their complaints was when Delilah played the conch shell for them. Then they would all go quiet. Their pupils would dilate, and they would stare off at nothing with blank expressions on their faces. Their jaws would drop open. Occasionally they drooled. That was when Delilah was happiest.

"After several days, Delilah noticed that the men were dying. It was the heat. Delilah—being very small and resilient—managed the heat quite as well as the birds and the monkeys and the snakes. But no adult human could survive it for very long. The sailors would not eat. They lay on the ground and panted. To soothe them, Delilah played the conch shell constantly. As ill as they were, it still be-witched the sailors. It bewitched the dying cells within their bodies too.

"Now, cells are very passionate things. They love a good time. And the sailor's cells knew that if the sailors died, they would no longer be able to enjoy Delilah's music. So the cells did the only sensible thing. They mutated. They bumped and bounced and twisted until the dying sailors gradually turned into creatures that could survive the heat of the island. They became lizards."

"Lizards!" Olivia cried, and thought of the lizards that crawled all over Sidi. She held her hand to her mouth to keep from shrieking out loud.

"Oh, yes," Johansson said. "As lizards they survived quite well. Of course, they were not very good conversationalists. For two or three months after the sailors turned into lizards, they were still able to talk a little bit, but they gradually lost their powers of speech until they were just plain old lizards.

"So Delilah had to pick up the conch shell and play her song to the ocean again. Sure enough, people would appear out on the horizon, swimming with all their heart to Delilah's island. They were not always sailors. Some of them were cruise ship aerobics instructors or stockbrokers

who had been sailing their yachts, or once, a hundred and seven refugees who had been floating for days on a raft. Some say that Master Clive was among the people who swam to Delilah, and that she exacted her revenge on him in a particularly brutal way.

"All different kinds of people came to Delilah's island, called by her conch shell. But it was always the same in the end. They always turned into lizards. Years passed. Delilah turned into a young woman. Many of the men who swam ashore fell in love with her. She assured them that it was hopeless, that they would turn into a lizard within the week. Of course, they didn't believe her and pestered her for kisses. Finally she made them a deal: The first man who did not turn into a lizard after the first week would be the man whom she would marry. The men thought it was likely she was insane, but they reasoned that they would take her to a psychiatrist once they got her off the island. Which none of them ever did since they all became lizards by the end of the week.

"It was a television news crew who saved Delilah in the end. A little more than a month ago they were investigating a story on the mysterious disappearances of people who sailed on the waters around the Hydrocophegene Islands. When they found Delilah, she was no longer young.

Her hair had turned silver and hung down to the back of her knees, and there were lizards tangled within it. Lizards were draped over her strong shoulders and riding on her toes like jewels.

" 'Do you know who I think this woman is?' a cameraman from the television crew whispered excitedly to the gaffer.

" 'Who?'

" 'I think she is Sidi! The teenage pilot whose plane disappeared during her round-the-world flight.'

" 'But that was more than forty-five years ago,' the gaffer said. 'And I thought Sidi's plane crashed into the ocean and she died.'

" 'That is what people speculated. But no one ever found the plane or Sidi. And besides,' said the cameraman, 'we failed to solve the mystery of all those people who have disappeared off their boats. We had better come back with *something* interesting or we'll be fired.'

"So they rescued Delilah from the island, even indulging her wish to take all her lizards with her. Her return to New York City was greeted with great fanfare—for in everyone's eyes she was not Delilah, but the remarkable Sidi. She took on Sidi's name and came to live here. Only a few weeks ago, there were parades and reporters and people sending flowers. But that all died down, as she knew that it would. You see, Sidi (I, too, call her Sidi now) is still as wise as she was when she was little Delilah, the cook's daughter. Loyalty, she knows, rarely lasts. Except among lizards. So she keeps them alive as best she can. Oh, the heating bills are astronomical! But we survive by the small tokens that people give to hear Sidi play on the conch shell. Money, jewelry. Even books. And now . . . I'm sure you will not wish to deny Sidi such a little token to hear her sweet music. Why, people have swum across miles of ocean for the pleasure."

Olivia considered this remarkable story in the silence that followed. Then she said, "I feel sorry for her." She meant it too. She knew there was nothing in the world worse than loneliness. "It must have been horrible for her on that island. But I'm sorry for Delilah, not for Sidi. I don't like Sidi. She's greedy, and by the way, she does not treat you very nicely either. She can't have my book, or anything else of mine. I feel much better now, thank you. And now I'm going back inside to speak to my father," she said firmly, and slipped her arms through her knapsack straps. Bracing herself for the heat, she opened the terrace door and immediately heard the most bloodcurdling scream.

Ten

Sidi was screaming and holding a lizard by its tail as it dangled upside down and pawed at the air.

"Aaaiiiiiich!! He has bitten me!" she shrieked at Johansson.

"Hey, Buster!" the lizard said as it struggled to right itself. It was the same lizard that Olivia had kicked off her sneaker.

"Kill him, Johansson!" Sidi ordered. "I will not have a biter!" The other lizards crawled nervously over her body.

The lizard's voice was definitely that of a human man, and a very angry human man at that. Olivia guessed that he couldn't have been a lizard for very long or he would have lost his voice by now.

Johansson took the lizard from Sidi's fingers and began to walk back out to the terrace.

"But you can't kill him," Olivia protested. "He used to be a man. That's . . . well, that's murder."

"Hmmm." Johansson looked at her contemplatively. He nodded his head. "Quite right, quite right. Hold this a moment, please." He put the poor, struggling lizard into Olivia's hand and left the room. She held him, not knowing what else to do, cupping one hand over the other and spreading her fingers a little so that he could get air. She felt his tiny feet scrambling across her hand as he tried to find a way out of the little prison.

He will probably bite me, Olivia thought. But to her surprise the lizard began to relax. He stopped moving about and she felt his cool, smooth belly expand and contract against her palm, slower and slower. "Hey, Buster," she heard him murmur as though he were falling asleep.

I guess he feels safe with me, Olivia thought. It was a very satisfying sensation. She kept her hand as steady as possible so as not to disturb him.

When Johansson returned, he was carrying something black and shiny in one hand. It took Olivia a moment to realize what it was: a pair of black rubber gloves. He put them on. They were too large for him—the tips of the fingers flopped down and his wrists stuck out from the bottom like the clapper in a bell.

"Murder is always messier than one would imagine," Johansson explained to Olivia, appearing a little embarrassed.

"Master Clive!" Olivia gasped. Johansson bowed cavalierly.

"The very one," he replied.

"But . . . Master Clive was, was—"

"A large menacing chap?" Johansson sighed. "Yes. That was many, many years ago. Before I heard the lovely siren call and jumped ship. Before I swam miles in the cold, tossing ocean toward the most beautiful, heartbreaking music I had ever heard. When I came ashore, I didn't recognize the cook's daughter. But *she* recognized *me*. Later she told me she had intended to turn me into a lizard and feed me to a snake. But as I told you before, Master Clive has a very strong constitution. Her music diminished me, yes. I shrank and dwindled away into this." He brushed a gloved hand in front of his body. "But I would not *turn*, Master Clive would *not* turn. So," he concluded, "she made me into her servant instead. Which, all in all, is a fair punishment, I suppose, for the pleasure of strangling her father. He had a very soft neck, you see, and it felt like kneading cake dough . . . very delightful!" He smiled at Olivia and she saw the cruelty break across his face. Suddenly Olivia remembered the words of the old lady in the glass apartment:

"The most dangerous people are those who appear most harmless."

"Now, miss." He came closer to her. "The lizard, please." Olivia backed up, keeping her hand tightly cupped.

"No," she said. He grabbed at her and she leapt away. But still he kept advancing, the shiny black gloves outstretched, their cold, slick touch only inches away from her throat. Cornered, she sidled along the wall until she reached the terrace door. She opened it and stepped outside. He followed her, closing the terrace door gently behind him.

"We must keep out the cold," he said genially. Within her palms, the lizard had woken up and she felt him poking his head uneasily out between her fingers.

"Hey, Buster," he whispered fearfully.

"It's all right," Olivia whispered into her fist. "I won't let him hurt you." She felt the little lizard calm down. Through the terrace window, a familiar head appeared in Sidi's parlor—a rumple of sandy brown hair. A tall man with a bouncy, rubbery gait. Her father! He was carrying a red toolbox and speaking to Sidi, who was smiling and nodding her head.

"Daddy!" she cried out in joy. He would know what to do! He would talk to Master Clive in his easy, friendly way.

He would make the situation all right. And then Olivia could go home, where things were safe and solid. She held the lizard securely in one hand and waved through the terrace window with the other.

"Daddy, I'm here!" Olivia called. Master Clive cocked his head at her as if she were a curious and amusing zoo animal.

"How charming children are. How foolish," he said. "He can't hear you, my dear. Our parlor is soundproof. We must have our privacy, you understand." Olivia screamed even louder, but her father did not even look her way. She watched as he turned and began to walk out of the parlor, out of the apartment.

Olivia swallowed back the hard clot of terror that was beginning to form in her throat. She looked at Master Clive. There was something truly overpowering in his expression—a gruesome hunger for brutality. It made her tremble.

"You know, my dear," said Master Clive, "every year, in this city, one or two children tumble off a terrace and fall to their death. It is a most unhappy ordeal for everyone. The parents are unhappy. The child's friends are unhappy. And the child is most certainly unhappy! Naughty, naughty children. Playing where they should not be playing. Now give me that lizard at once and we shall see what we can do about keeping you alive. Perhaps, if you are a good girl, Sidi will play you into a delightful stupor. You will be grinning from ear to ear like that other child in there. Gretchen, I believe her name is. Why, that girl was perfectly brilliant when she first came to us. Brilliant and unhappy. Now she is happy. A happy idiot. Nothing wrong with that. We only have to take care not to let her turn into a lizard. Come, my dear." He put out his hand. "It would be a pity to make your father scrape you off the pavement."

Out of the corner of her eye, Olivia spied the terrace belonging to the apartment directly below. It was piled high with junk—stacks of old clothing, parts of bicycles, bags of garbage. It was a good six-foot drop, but she would have to fall down and in toward the building. If she simply fell straight down, she would only graze the outside of the terrace railing below and then fall six stories to the sidewalk. But there was no other choice at the moment. It was the only way. Swiftly she hauled one leg up over the terrace railing, then the other leg. Her toes balanced along the edge of the terrace and she clung to the railing with one hand, the other still holding the lizard. She looked down at the shiny cars passing beneath her, thinking how small the people on the street were.

"You won't make it," Master Clive said. She knew he was right because he looked too happy. He had stepped back away from the edge and was smiling blissfully. She would not fall onto the terrace below but would miss it by inches. She thought about her poor father. She thought of all the difficulties he had been through. Now his heart would finally be broken. The cold was beginning to bite painfully into her bare hands. She felt the lizard's breathing begin to quicken against her skin. She looked up one more time at Master Clive. He folded his arms and leaned back against the terrace door, waiting. She closed her eyes and let go.

Eleven

The hands that grabbed her waist were small and freckled. The hands that grabbed her knees were a little bigger and freckled. And the hands that gave her a reassuring squeeze on her shoulder belonged to Branwell. The two smaller boys had stacked themselves up, feet on shoulders just like in the circus, and had caught Olivia a moment after she let go of Sidi's terrace. Now the terrace that had been piled high with garbage was also piled high with active, freckled Biffmeyer children. The ones who had not stacked themselves up were scrambling over the piles of garbage, excited about this new game of catching falling people from the terraces above.

Olivia was gently lowered to the ground, where the Biffmeyer children crowded around her, staring at her with their bold, blue eyes.

"Can we keep her?" one of the girls asked, nibbling on an apple.

"She's not a pet," Branwell said. "Now give her a little room."

"How did you know?" Olivia asked. She had plopped down on a Hefty bag full of a soft substance, trying to regain some measure of composure.

"We heard you yelling for your father," said one of the boys. He had an extraordinary set of freckles that splayed across his upper lip, giving him the appearance of having a mustache.

"I knew it was you," said Branwell. "And you sounded like you were in a mess of trouble. What were you doing?"

Olivia stood up and craned her neck back to see the terrace above them. Master Clive was gone. It was as if he had never been there at all. She looked at her closed fist, then slowly opened it. She almost expected to see an empty hand, but no, the lizard was still there. He looked up at her with his round, yellow eyes and blinked. Olivia was so relieved, she smiled down at him.

"Hey, Buster," she said to the lizard fondly.

"A lizard!" one of the Biffmeyer boys shouted, and he made a grab for it. The little lizard jumped out of Olivia's hand and scuttered underneath the terrace door into the Biffmeyers' apartment.

Olivia cried out in alarm, but Branwell said, "Don't worry. Animals get treated very well here."

"Hey," said the boy with the freckle mustache. "It's rotten cold out here. Don't you have a coat or something?"

"I left it upstairs," Olivia said, taking a mental inventory of the things she had left in her coat pocket: half a pack of watermelon bubble gum, a hair barrette shaped like a chili pepper, some change—but not a whole lot—and a note from Ms. Dart to her father. (She had opened it, even though she wasn't supposed to, and read the short note: "Despite our sessions, Olivia still persists in her delusions. Although her fantasies may be normal for a child who has experienced the sort of trauma that Olivia has experienced, it does seem to be interfering with her schoolwork. I think we should begin to consider medication.") Well, her coat and all the items in it were gone for good. There was no way she would ever return to Sidi's apartment to fetch them. She was a little sorry about the barrette, but now she would not have to worry about giving the note to her father either. And at least she had managed to keep her knapsack.

"Come on inside and warm up," said Branwell. "Meet our mom. You'll like her." He opened the terrace door and Freckle Mustache jumped back as if it surprised him.

"Didn't you tell Mom to call the super about fixing this door, Lottie?" Freckle Mustache asked one of the bigger girls.

"You can tell her as well as me," she protested. Olivia could see nothing in particular wrong with the door, but she supposed that with so many kids, things would always be breaking. She walked in the apartment and all the Biffmeyer children followed, jumping and bouncing and ricocheting off each other like a pan of heated popcorn.

It was a messy apartment, with clothes and toys and books concealing every surface. There must have been furniture, but all Olivia could make out were stacks of clutter that were shaped a little like a chair or a table. No matter. The temperature in the apartment was absolutely perfect. Not too hot, not too cold. Human temperature. She had never appreciated temperature before. She took in a deep breath of contentment. It was a stranger's home, and she was not generally comfortable in apartments other than her own. But this afternoon she had found herself in so *many* strangers' apartments that she believed she was almost getting used to it. And so far, this one was her favorite. It was messy, yes, but it looked normal. No glass floors, no murderous pirates.

Still, there was an odor. She noticed it right away but could not identify it. It broke against her nostrils in sour little bursts and was so strong that she could actually taste it on her tongue. From the interior of the apartment came a low, gurgling noise.

"We were just in the middle of Charlie-in-a-Jam when we heard you screaming," Branwell said. "Actually we were supposed to be doing our chores, but in this house nothing ever gets done straight."

"What's Charlie-in-a-Jam?" Olivia asked.

"Oh, that's right!" Lottie cried. "We never finished our game!" Immediately all the children began to poke around under piles of clutter, opening cabinets, checking the closets, then dispersing down the hallway in a fit of howls and shrieks.

"Want to meet my mom?" Branwell asked when they were alone. It was funny the way he was so eager for her to meet his mother. Most kids she knew were embarrassed of their parents and tried to keep their friends from having any contact with them. But Branwell seemed so proud of his mother that it made Olivia curious.

"Sure," she said, and followed Branwell down the hall. It was an L-shaped hallway, and as they hooked around the corner, the sour odor grew strong. They passed a bathroom and Olivia wondered if maybe the toilet was broken and that was the source of the smell, but no. It came from the last room, the room that Branwell entered.

"Here she is," he said, presenting his mother as though she were the most exquisite and fascinating person either one of them could ever hope to meet. The woman in question did not look up at first. She was too busy at her task of milking a small, cranky goat. The silver and black animal squirmed and kicked while the woman managed to squeeze out a thin stream of milk into a pail. Half a dozen chickens marched around the woman's feet, coming within kicking distance of the sharp little goat hooves without ever getting kicked. Perched clumsily on top of a television set was a large turkey. It watched Olivia with keen, dark eyes, then flew to the roof of a wooden lean-to in which a short, fat donkey was minding its own business.

"Hi," Olivia said when it looked as if she might stand there forever without being acknowledged. The woman looked up from her seat on a low stool. She looked a little like an owl. She wore wire-rimmed glasses over a pair of large round eyes. Her skin looked very soft and was, amazingly, completely unfreckled. There was something so comforting about her, so *motherly*. Olivia thought wistfully about how nice it would be to have a mother like that.

Mrs. Biffmeyer looked at Olivia quizzically, then smiled. Her smile was very sweet and a little confused. Olivia wished that Branwell would say something to break the ice, but he wouldn't.

"I'm Olivia."

"Hello, Olivia," Mrs. Biffmeyer said. "Are you a friend of Lottie's?"

"I'm Branwell's friend," Olivia replied. It was funny to say that. She had certainly never considered Branwell a friend before today. But as the words came out of her mouth, she knew they were true.

"Branwell?" The woman cocked her head.

"Your son," Olivia said. "Branwell."

"Oh! Okay." Mrs. Biffmeyer rolled her eyes to the ceiling for a moment, nodding her head. "There are so many children and animals, you see. It gets a little . . . overwhelming. Mmm. Hmm. Branwell. The children make up the strangest nicknames for themselves!" The little goat began to fidget, and Mrs. Biffmeyer excused herself and resumed her task.

How could a mother forget her own child!? The

thought infuriated Olivia! She readjusted her first impression and decided that she didn't like Mrs. Biffmeyer after all. It was stupid to have so many children that you couldn't remember them all. She looked over at Branwell, fully prepared to be outraged on his behalf. But he didn't seem bothered at all. He smiled at her lightly.

"Isn't she great?" he said.

The sudden sound of bedlam—childish screams and yelps—erupted from somewhere.

"Someone must have won Charlie-in-a-Jam! Come on." Branwell grabbed Olivia's hand and they ran down the hallway toward the noise. No boy had ever held Olivia's hand before. Not counting her father and her brother, of course. To her surprise, she didn't really mind it. His hand looked rough, but his skin felt cool and his touch was weightless—like cupping wind.

Twelve

As it turned out, the screams were not coming from within the apartment. They were coming from the hallway outside. More precisely, from the tiny incinerator room where people on the floor went to throw their garbage down the metal chute. All the Biffmeyer children surrounded the incinerator room, jumping and squealing. Among the squeals, however, was the sound of real panic. A child's howling.

"Oh, no," said Branwell. "Not again." He walked quickly to the little group, Olivia trailing just behind him. Branwell slipped in between his brothers and sisters, into the incinerator room.

"What's going on?" Olivia asked.

"Charlie got put into the incinerator chute again," said Freckle Mustache. Indeed Olivia could now see that the incinerator chute hatch was open and that a dark-haired head was sticking out of it. The rest of his body appeared to have been stuffed into the chute.

"Oh, poor thing!" Olivia said. "Why would someone do that to him?"

"Because that's the game," explained one of the girls a little defensively. "Charlie-in-a-Jam. One of us jams Charlie into something and the rest of us have to find him." Olivia guessed that this little girl was the one who had jammed him into the chute.

"Pull him out by his hair!" one of them suggested.

"I'm trying, but he keeps screaming!" said another. Olivia nudged her way in to get a closer look. It seemed to her that Charlie was wedged in there pretty tightly, like a bag of garbage that was stuffed too full. The little boy was alternately sobbing and twisting his body to try to escape. The more he twisted, the more securely he became wedged in the chute.

"How about if we just push him *down* the chute," said Freckle Mustache.

"But the incinerator furnace might be on when he hits the bottom," said Lottie. "Then he'd burn up."

At this, Charlie began to wail, "No, no, not down! Not down!"

"They only turn on the furnace in the morning," said Freckle Mustache.

"No, you dope. They turn it on in the afternoon," argued Lottie. And the argument escalated while Branwell tried to soothe Charlie by whispering things into his ear. But the little boy was inconsolable, and he persisted in turning and turning until the decision of what to do with Charlie came to an abrupt end. Charlie managed to unwedge his body and suddenly slipped down the incinerator chute and disappeared. All they could hear was his wailing becoming softer and softer as he descended through the garbage shaft, until finally it was gone.

Thirteen

For a moment or two, all any of them could do was look at each other with wide eyes.

"I hope I'm wrong," Lottie said quietly.

"We'd better go down and see for ourselves," Freckle Mustache said solemnly. At the mention of activity the Biffmeyer children became rowdy again. Action was their element, and too impatient for the elevator, they whooped and hollered and started down the stairs in a mad, wild race. Branwell stayed back to wait for the elevator, and Olivia, not eager to be caught in the middle of a Biffmeyer riot, stayed with him.

"I keep telling them not to play that game. They just don't listen to me. It's like they don't even hear me. Poor Charlie." Branwell's face was pinched with worry now.

"I bet he'll be okay," Olivia said.

"It's hard being the youngest," Branwell said. Olivia thought about that for a minute.

"I'm the youngest," she said.

The elevator door opened. There was no one else in there. Branwell pushed B for basement. Olivia looked at him. It was so strange that she didn't recognize him from English class.

"What do you do on Tuesdays at ten forty-five?" Branwell asked suddenly.

"What?"

"Every Tuesday at ten forty-five you get up and leave class," Branwell said. "Where do you go?" Olivia pressed the B button several times as though it could make the elevator go faster. She considered several answers to his questions, but they were all lies. She didn't mind lying once in a while. But she didn't feel like lying to Branwell.

"I go to see Ms. Dart. The school psychiatrist," Olivia said. He nodded thoughtfully.

"What's she like?" he asked. Olivia was thankful that he didn't ask what was "wrong" with her.

"Her perfume makes me a little dizzy. And she licks her lips so much that it looks like she's thinking of food all the time. But she's fine, I guess."

The elevator stopped at the basement and Olivia rushed out, partly to see what had happened to Charlie and partly to get away from the conversation. The incinerator was past a series of heavy metal doors and through a maze of hallways.

Olivia opened the furnace door and there was Charlie, sitting in the square, metal incinerator, unharmed except for a few scratches, a coating of black soot, and a nasty odor of garbage on him. Branwell looked very relieved.

The sound of a dozen or so sneakers pounding on the stairs gave way to the creak of the stairwell door. The Biffmeyers came running over to the furnace, breathless and crying, "Is he burned up? Is he burned up?" They didn't sound the least bit terrified. In fact they seemed a little disappointed to find that nothing very dramatic had happened to poor Charlie. He looked a little dazed at his predicament, but already the Biffmeyer in him was rearing its fearless spirit.

"That was fun. Can I do it again?" Charlie said. This lifted his siblings' mood, and they shouted for another round of Charlie-in-a-Jam. No wonder it was such a popular game. Why not, when Charlie was so willing to be jammed?

"Hey, you guys, be careful. Don't hurt him!" Branwell warned. But they rushed by him without paying any attention, and hustled Charlie back up the stairs.

They were alone again and Olivia suddenly began to feel a little strange with Branwell. They were silent for a moment. She felt like he wanted to tell her something, but she was not sure she wanted to know.

"Olivia," he began, "did you know there is a floor beneath this one?"

"No there's not," Olivia snapped back. He had made her nervous, and whenever she was nervous, she grew snippy. "This is the basement. *B*. B is for basement. Bottom. It's the last button on the elevator."

"There's a subbasement under this," Branwell said. "The elevator doesn't go there. You have to take the stairs. Will you come with me?" His voice was so serious that she felt a small chill run through her body. It wasn't fear. After her encounter with Master Clive she wasn't likely to be so easily scared. But she felt like something important was about to happen, as if the next few moments would change things. In the past few months her life had changed so much. If she couldn't make it change back, at least she could prevent it from changing even more.

"I don't think I want to," she said. "I think I'm going

back to the twelfth floor. I think I'm going to wait outside my apartment door and read a book until my father comes home."

"The book on séances?" Branwell asked. Olivia frowned at him, as if he were making fun of her.

"Why do they make you go see Ms. Dart on Tuesdays at ten forty-five, Olivia?" There was no maliciousness in his voice. He asked the question in the same way that her father sometimes asked who she was talking to when she was alone in her room. Branwell sounded concerned. He sounded like he might even listen.

"Because I talk to myself sometimes."

"Everyone does that," Branwell said.

"But I'm *not* talking to myself," Olivia said. "I'm talking to someone else."

"Who?"

"My brother. Christopher."

"I don't understand," Branwell said.

Olivia hesitated, swallowed. "Christopher is dead. He died three months ago."

"Oh." Branwell nodded. Olivia searched his expression for shock or disgust or ridicule. But there was no surprise at all. "Does he answer back?" Branwell asked. That was the one question no one ever asked her. Not Ms. Dart or the principal or her father. That was the one question that con-sumed Olivia's thoughts day and night. She shook her head.

"Never."

"And you're afraid that means he's nothing now? Van-ished? Like steam disappearing into the air?"

Olivia nodded. Branwell didn't offer any reassuring words. He didn't say things like the minister at the funeral: "Christopher's spirit will always be with us." Or like the nurses in the cancer ward where Christopher was hospi-talized: "His body is just a shell that's grown too fragile." Instead, Branwell took her hand.

"Come with me downstairs," he said again. His voice was pleading.

"Okay," she said.

Fourteen

They took the stairs down. It was not the same stairwell that was used for the rest of the building, but a hidden set of stairs you got to by entering what looked to be a broom closet. The stairwell was small and dark, and the stairs themselves were old and crumbling. Olivia could feel the cold dampness of the walls. The air grew colder and colder as they descended. At the landing was a heavy wooden door. Branwell pulled it open with some difficulty, its edges having warped and swelled with age. As the door opened, a rush of moldy, chilly air hit their faces, and they stepped inside.

The subbasement was very dark, so it took a minute for Olivia's eyes to adjust. Gradually, as the darkness lifted, she could make out a large, low-ceilinged room with a maze of pipes running across the ceiling and nothing much else. In fact it would have been completely unremarkable except for a tall cylindrical object that stood smack in the center of the room.

Olivia walked up to it. It was made of brick and, from the look of it, was very old. It was quite tall too, nearly reaching the ceiling, and wider than her outstretched arms. A thick layer of grime dulled the color of the brick, and along the top, the bricks were loose and falling apart.

"What is it?" she asked. In the empty, cavernous room her voice rang hollow, like the only sound on a cold, abandoned planet.

"I keep wondering the same thing." Branwell's voice also sounded odd, dreamy.

"It gives me a funny feeling," she confessed.

"I know. Me too," Branwell said. "I feel like something important happened here. I don't know what. But every time I'm feeling sad about things, I come down here."

"Does it help?" There was a long pause, so long that Olivia turned to Branwell to see if he had heard her. In the darkness his face was filmy, blurred. He seemed all hair and eyes while his pale skin retreated into the shadows.

"Sometimes I feel like I'm trying to find something," Branwell said. "I'm not sure what. But when I come down here, I feel like I've found what I was looking for. I feel relieved, happy. But as soon as I start back home again, that feeling of sadness returns."

It bothered Olivia a lot that Branwell could feel such sadness. She herself had felt sadness for so long that she had hardly ever considered that others might feel it too. Now she suddenly thought of her father. Surely Christopher's death must have been awful for him. But he didn't show it. Or else Olivia had failed to notice it. Her father's face always seemed so full of joy.

"I tried to talk to my mother about it once," Branwell said. "But, you know, with all the kids and animals . . ." He didn't finish, but Olivia could imagine his mother not paying any attention to the son whose name she couldn't even remember.

"You said it's hard to be the youngest kid in the family," Olivia said. "But I bet it's even harder being the oldest. Especially with all those brothers and sisters."

"Not really." Branwell's voice brightened at the mention of his wild siblings. "Mostly it's fun. I just feel so responsible for all of them. I feel like if I don't keep an eye on them all the time, they'll get themselves into trouble."

"They seem to do that even while you *do* keep an eye

on them!" Olivia laughed and so did Branwell, and each was glad that the somber mood had lifted.

Suddenly they heard footsteps on the stairs. They stared at each other in the dark, their eyes wide.

"Do people come down here?" Olivia whispered.

"No one."

"Ever?"

"Never." They waited as the footsteps grew louder. At each step a metal clanking could be heard.

Olivia instantly recalled the old ghost stories that she heard at slumber parties. There was always a ghost with a chain tethered to its legs that clanked as it walked. Her breath grew quick and shallow as she struggled to remain calm. She looked in the darkness toward Branwell, but suddenly she could no longer see him. He must have drawn off to a dark corner, to hide from the intruder. She did the same, running around behind the brick cylinder, and together they waited to see who would open the door.

Fifteen

The intruder opened the door quite easily. Olivia heard the bottom of the door scrape against the ground, and then more footsteps, accompanied by the menacing metallic clang. Olivia tried to keep her breathing as silent as possible, although her heart was beating so hard, she was sure it could be heard. The footsteps came closer, approaching the cylinder. She wondered, with horror, if it was Master Clive. Perhaps he had followed them down here. She began to tremble and pressed her face against the cold brick. For a moment she closed her eyes, wanting to block out what might be coming. No, she decided. No! She was going to keep her eyes open and her mind alert. No matter what. But that clanging was so frightening. It came closer and closer as the intruder made its way around the circumference of the structure. As the clanging grew close,

Olivia backed away, circling around until she was once more facing the subbasement door.

I can make a run for it, she thought. But then she remembered Branwell. No, she decided, I won't leave him here alone. Olivia stayed where she was. She would face him, even if it *was* Master Clive with his black rubber gloves. Having Branwell close by made her feel bold.

The clanging was so close now that Olivia had to squeeze her toes against the soles of her shoes to keep from running away. A shadowy figure appeared from around the cylinder and stopped a few feet in front of her. It was shaped in the form of a man. It reached up its arm and rubbed the top of its head. She saw its head tilt to one side. It seemed to be looking right at her.

"Olivia?" it said.

"Dad?" She actually smelled him even before she made out his familiar features. He had a distinct smell of caulking glue and bitter-orange hand cleaner. She ran to him, propelled herself, really, against him. He caught her and clanged slightly. The clanging, she discovered, was coming from the side of his belt where a large ring of keys hung by a hook. Their own house keys were among them—the keys that she had been trying to get hold of all afternoon. Now they didn't seem so important.

"What are you doing down here, Dad?"

"I was looking for the boiler room. What are *you* doing down here, Sweetpea?" Olivia could hear that edge of concern creep into her father's voice. Lately he was always watching her for signs of strangeness.

"I'm here with a friend," she said, glad to relieve him of his fears. "Branwell!" she called into the darkness. "It's okay. It's just my dad!" They waited, but there was only silence.

"He hid when he heard you coming," Olivia explained to her dad. George Kidney reached for his tool belt and pulled out a flashlight. He shot the bright beam throughout the room, from one end to the other. There was no sign of Branwell. He'd deserted her. She hadn't deserted him. Scared as she was, she didn't run out on him. She never would have. Now she felt betrayed. Foolish. And most of all, angry. When she saw him in class tomorrow, she wouldn't speak to him. Not a word.

"Well," George said, "looks like it's just me and you." He was trying to keep his voice light and joking, but Olivia could hear the worry in it. That made her even angrier at Branwell. He had made her look like a liar, or worse, crazy. She thought about the note in her coat pocket. Even if her father never saw it, Ms. Dart was sure to give him a call eventually. Then they'd discuss giving Olivia medication. Perhaps her father would think it was a good idea.

"Maybe he slipped by you when you came in," Olivia suggested.

"Maybe," Mr. Kidney said doubtfully. "Hey, honey, let's go home. I've had the longest day. You know, when you go inside people's apartments, you find out a lot of things that you'd rather not know."

Sixteen

They made a meat loaf for dinner. Olivia and her father used to always make dinner together when Olivia's mother was still living with them. Before the divorce. Her mother hated to cook, or rather she hated the smells of cooking food. If Mrs. Kidney cooked a meal, she simply could not eat it—the odor nauseated her too much. And if she could not eat, she said, she was no good for anyone. So George cooked all the meals and Olivia hung around him until she learned to cook nearly as well as George. Together they had cooked some extravagant things—salmon in cream sauce and chicken cordon bleu; braised asparagus, pear tarts. But since her mother had left, packed up her things one day, including all the dolls, and went out to California to make jewelry, Olivia and her father had stopped fixing fancy dinners. Somehow it just wasn't worth it anymore.

Then Christopher died and it seemed like Olivia and her father had stopped eating with each other altogether. Usually, by the time her father came home from work, Olivia had already eaten her dinner. And although George offered to cook her breakfast in the mornings, Olivia always declined, grabbing a few slices of toast to eat on the way to school. Suddenly she realized how much she missed those old times with him.

"How was school today?" George asked while they were having dinner.

"Good," Olivia lied.

"Hey, you know," he said brightly, "there's a whole lot of kids living in this building."

"Most of them are Biffmeyers."

"What's a Biffmeyer?" George asked. That made Olivia laugh, which pleased George to no end. Although he was in his forties, he sometimes looked just like a teenage boy, all rubbery and awkward and silly.

"It's nice to see you laugh, Olivia," George said. "We used to laugh a lot, didn't we—you, me, and Christopher?" Olivia nodded. For a minute they were silent.

"I miss him," Olivia said finally. She felt herself tearing up and frowned hard, trying to bear down on the pain.

"Me too," George said. "Me too." Olivia looked at her

father. His eyes were damp. In them she saw her own grief reflected back at her. Why had she not noticed this before? She realized that she had not looked in her father's eyes since Christopher's death. Not once. All this time she had been afraid to look at him too closely. She carried so much sadness inside her that she sometimes thought she would crack in two; there just hadn't been any extra room in her heart to know about her father's sadness too. But today—on this strange and puzzling day—she could look at him. And instead of breaking in two, she felt oddly relieved.

"Do you know what we haven't done for the longest time?" she asked. George wiped his damp eyes on his wrists and shook his head.

"What?"

"We haven't made brownies," Olivia said.

"Fudge brownies."

"With walnuts?"

"Crammed with walnuts!"

After dinner they dug out a box of brownie mix from the pantry. In the old days they would have made it from scratch, but now a mix seemed just fine. They opened a bag of walnuts and were having such fun cracking the nuts open that they wound up using three times the amount that the recipe called for. After they poured the mix into a pan and popped it in the oven, George checked his watch.

"It takes twenty minutes to bake," he said. "Let's see, it's almost seven o'clock now . . ."

Seven o'clock. Seven o'clock? There was something about seven o'clock that was important. Oh! The séance! Madame Brenda! Olivia hesitated. She considered whether she really wanted to go. If what Alice had said was true—that Madame Brenda could summon almost any spirit—then wouldn't she be able to summon Christopher? Not only would Olivia be able to talk *to* her brother, but he would finally talk *back*. He could tell her if he was okay. He could tell her where he was now and what it was like. Whether he had friends, and whether he still thought about her and Dad. Whether he heard all the things she told him.

"Dad," Olivia said finally, "I'm going downstairs to a friend's house."

"What about the brownies?" George asked. He sounded so disappointed.

"I'll be back soon, I promise," Olivia said. "Keep the brownies warm for me."

Seventeen

When Olivia arrived at Alice's apartment, Madame Brenda was already there. She was not at all what Olivia had expected. Madame Brenda sat at a little living room table, surrounded by a clutter of shoes and pocketbooks and shopping bags from Lord & Taylor and Bloomingdale's. Dressed in a billowy pink sweater and pink slacks, she was an older woman, but didn't appear elderly (certainly not a hundred years old, as Alice had said). Her hair was dyed a tomato red, and she had a large black beauty mark on her cheek. She wore large glasses with candy-red frames that were attached to a chain around her neck, and at the moment, she was gazing through them, examining her purchases.

"Now these"—Madame Brenda held up a pair of blue heels—"were on sale, plus I got them to take fifteen percent off for the tiniest little scratch on the toe. Can you believe the salesgirl accused me of scratching it myself with my keys!" She blinked very slowly, with great indignation. Her eyelids were shadowed with a sparkly green. "And what if I *had* scratched it with my keys? Who would want a shoe with a scratch on it? They should be thankful that I bought them! Thankful!"

Olivia's heart sank. So this was Madame Brenda. She looked like someone's eccentric grandmother who spent winters in Florida and married a succession of rich men with leathery tans. It seemed very unlikely that this woman would have mystical powers of any kind except to divine where the ladies' bathroom was in Macy's.

Alice, on the other hand, did not seem at all disappointed. In honor of her renowned guest, she had traded her housedress for a worn but clean denim jumper and had combed her hair. She looked no more remarkable now than she had earlier, but at least she tried. She was listening intently as Madame Brenda sifted through the rest of her shoes and bags, going over all the sales and bargains and harmless swindles that she had played on the snooty salesgirls.

On seeing Olivia, his savior, little Patrick ran over to her and she lifted him in her arms. As he clung there, his head swiveled toward Madame Brenda. He seemed a little afraid of her and Olivia didn't blame him. But the events of this afternoon had made Olivia brave. And impatient with nonsense.

"Excuse me," Olivia interrupted. "I came for a séance, not for a fashion show." Madame Brenda stopped talking immediately. She looked over at Olivia, staring at her over the top of her glasses, as if she were seeing her now for the first time.

"And *I*," said Madame Brenda, "came all the way from Miami Beach, where, incidentally, the temperature is seventy-eight degrees, to New York City in the middle of winter. So excuse *me*"—Madame Brenda's voice was as raspy as a man with a sore throat—"if I do a little shopping on the way. I didn't know it was a *crime*. And by the way, darling, your brother, Christopher, is busy at the moment. So unless you want me to interrupt him, I think we can wait on the séance until I have a little snack and maybe a nice beverage?" She addressed this to Alice, who immediately rushed toward the kitchen to fetch a snack and a beverage for the illustrious Madame Brenda.

Olivia stood with Patrick in her arms, stunned. How Madame Brenda could have possibly known about Christopher was a mystery. Olivia had certainly not mentioned him to Alice. And no one knew that she wanted to contact him in a séance.

"Come, darling," Madame Brenda beckoned to Olivia while Alice was in the kitchen. "Sit by me and be sociable." Patrick scrambled away as soon as Olivia came near Madame Brenda.

"What size hat do you wear, darling?" Madame Brenda asked. Olivia, of course, had no idea, but Madame Brenda insisted that Olivia model a few of her purchases. She plopped a half dozen different hats on Olivia's head, tipping them this way and that and finally decreeing that Olivia's head was too narrow for hats.

"I hope you are not narrow-minded as well, darling. I have a feeling that we will see some extraordinary things this evening. The spirits are clamoring tonight. Do you feel it, Alice!?" Madame Brenda called into the kitchen. "Do you feel that the spirits are restless tonight?"

Alice ducked her head out of the kitchen and agreed enthusiastically, "Oh, yes! Very restless!" then disappeared again.

"Poor woman. She has no psychic gifts at all," Madame Brenda confided in Olivia.

"Then why are you here?" Olivia asked. Suddenly Madame Brenda reached over and took Olivia's chin between her fingers. She looked hard into Olivia's face, then drew away without explanation.

"I'm here on business. Old business. I've been a psychic medium for many, many years. I won't tell you how many, darling, because I'm a little vain, and it's none of your business anyway. But as mediums go, I have been very successful. There are very few spirits that I cannot contact. Spirits, in general, like to chat and I am a very good listener. They chat, I listen, everyone is happy. But there have been a few . . ." Madame Brenda was temporarily diverted by Alice's offerings—a platter of sandwiches, a bowl of Chex Mix, and a tall glass of iced tea with a lemon wedge. Madame Brenda picked up a sandwich and peeled back the bread to find a smear of tuna salad. She put it back down distastefully and sipped at the iced tea. Alice looked a little crestfallen and sat down at the table.

"As I was saying, there have been one or two spirits that I just couldn't contact. Usually it's because the spirits don't realize they are actually dead. When I start to talk to them, they stick their fingers in their ears and go, 'yah, yah, yah, yah.' Well, not literally, but that's what it amounts to. It's very aggravating, let me tell you. One of those spirits has been haunting this apartment building for years and years, but I've never been able to do anything about it. He or she—I don't know which—pops up every so often and takes up residence in someone's apartment for a while. It's not sinister. It doesn't hurt anyone, but it gives folks the heebie-jeebies. Doors open and shut on their own. There are unexplained taps and bumps and footsteps. The usual fare. For a few years the ghost was pretty quiet and I thought we'd seen the last of it. But then I heard about the tapping in Alice's apartment. Well, I thought to myself, looks like our poor, confused spirit is back. So I figured I'd give it another try. Maybe this time I can convince it that it's dead. Also, the shoe sales are fabulous this time of year!"

"But why is it haunting *this* apartment building?" Alice asked. Olivia was sorely tempted to tell them that the ghost was nothing but a nosey old lady in apartment 12K, but she was afraid that Madame Brenda would call off the entire séance.

"Well, honey," Madame Brenda said, "I'm not completely sure. But spirits often haunt the places where their old homes used to be. Anytime a house is knocked down and a new one is put up in its place, that's when the circumstances are ripe for a haunting. Ever hear stories about a ghost walking through a wall? Well, most of the time it's because there used to be a door in that very spot, in the home they used to live in when they were alive. The ghost just thinks it's walking through the old doorway.

"This particular apartment building," Madame Brenda continued, "was built on top of the Berns family farm. They sold off their land in 1837, after some family tragedy occurred. My guess is that our ghost is a member of the Berns family and is probably connected to the tragedy." Olivia thought of the ancient-looking brick thing in the sub-basement.

"Okay!" Madame Brenda clapped her hands. "Are we ready to get down to business?" She cleared the little table of shoes and bags and hats and the platter of food. She kept her iced tea glass, however: "Talking to the dead dehydrates me something terrible."

"Should I turn off the lights?" Alice offered.

"Not unless you're having trouble paying your electric bills, darling. Now everyone hush." They all fell silent—even Patrick, who was sitting by Olivia's feet, toying with her shoelaces. Olivia wondered if the old lady upstairs was watching them all now. And smirking.

Eighteen

Olivia had expected some complicated chanting, lit candles, and the holding of hands. But instead Madame Brenda simply said, "Hello?"

They all listened. At first they didn't hear a single thing. Then suddenly there was a faint buzzing. It sounded like it could be some electrical appliance. Then Madame Brenda's face changed. The pupils of her eyes grew large, so large that her eyes appeared absolutely black.

"I hear you, Spirit," she said. "But you have to speak louder. Don't be shy. My name is Madame Brenda. Yes, darling, speak up, that's it. Oh!" Madame Brenda exclaimed suddenly. She frowned deeply and shook her head. "Marty, I told you for the last time! Don't disturb me when I'm working. What? What? Your lucky golf shirt? Oh, for goodness' sake, no. I haven't thrown it out. Now scram and let me do my work."

Madame Brenda turned to Alice and Olivia and explained, "My late husband, Marty. Such a pest. Okay, ladies, let's try again." She folded her hands on the table and once again addressed the air. "Hello?"

Nothing happened. Nothing at all. And then, very slowly, Madame Brenda's glass of iced tea floated up in the air. The lemon wedge that was perched on the side of the glass floated up too and was squeezed, by invisible hands, so that the lemon juice poured into the tea. Then slowly, the lemon fell back into the tea and the tea floated back down again, landing gently on the table. Olivia could not believe her eyes, and Alice was inhaling a long, wheezing breath of surprise. But Madame Brenda seemed nonchalant. She took a sip of her tea and said, "Thank you. Much better with the lemon in it. Now, may I ask your name?" They all waited. They didn't hear anything and apparently neither did Madame Brenda.

"It won't tell us its name," Madame Brenda explained to Olivia and Alice. "But it seems to want to communicate with us.

"If you are the spirit that lives in this apartment building, tap once for yes and twice for no." In a minute, there was a single tap. It startled Olivia, but then she wondered if the old lady upstairs was playing a trick on them. Her eyes flickered briefly upward, but they were met with nothing more than a cobweb in the corner.

"Excellent," said Madame Brenda. "Now I'm going to pick up a pen and I want you to guide my hand. Write down who you are and why you are here." Madame Brenda fished through her pocketbook for a pen and a pad of paper. "When spirits don't talk, sometimes they write," she explained. She held the pen to the paper and waited. Down on the floor, little Patrick was becoming bored or tired. In any case he had stopped playing with Olivia's shoelaces and was being very, very quiet.

Suddenly the pen began to move. Slowly and awkwardly at first. Then more and more quickly. It might simply have been Madame Brenda who was writing. But it *did* look as though her hand was simply hanging on to the pen as it moved across the paper. It stopped as suddenly as it had begun. Madame Brenda picked up the paper and this is what she read:

I can't talk too long. I've got lots of chores to do. The chickens need feeding and the barn has to be mucked out. Plus one of the cows is down with milk fever. Have you seen Johnny?

Madame Brenda looked at everyone and smiled. Then she gazed up at the air. "Who is Johnny, Spirit?" She put the pen to the paper and immediately her hand began to move. When it stopped, Madame Brenda read the next entry:

My brother, of course. He's supposed to help me with the barn. But he's always running off. Do you know where he is?

"No, Spirit, I do not," Madame Brenda said. "Do you know that you are dead, Spirit?" Once again the pen began to scribble across the paper. But this time the message was short:

I can't talk anymore. I have to go find my brother.

"You see," Madame Brenda said sadly to Olivia and Alice, "the spirit just stuck his fingers in his ears. Doesn't want to hear that he's dead. Poor thing. The ones that won't accept it have a hard time. They try to fit into this life, but they can't. People don't see them or hear them. They wind up feeling all alone and they don't know why. Oh, well, I tried." There was a squeal from beneath the table and everyone jumped, including Madame Brenda. Patrick crawled out, clutching something in his hand.

Nineteen

At first Olivia thought the long, skinny strand hanging from the bottom of Patrick's fist was her shoelace. Then she saw that it was actually a tail.

"Hey, Buster," it said.

"My lizard!" Olivia cried, and she opened Patrick's fist. The little lizard stared up at her. "Where did you find him, Patrick?"

Patrick pulled at the cuff of her pants. The lizard must have crawled in there back at the Biffmeyers' apartment and been traveling in her pant cuffs all this time. She was glad now for her big cuffs. She was also glad that he had come back to her, flattered even. She put out her hand and he crawled onto her palm.

"Hey, Buster," he said again.

"How strange!" Alice said. "It almost sounds like he said, 'Hey, Buster.' "

"He did."

"Oh. That's odd, that's so odd. You see . . ." Her eyes were growing teary and she wiped them quickly. "You see, my husband used to call Patrick 'Buster.' "

"Hey, Buster," the lizard said, and he crawled off Olivia's hand and onto the table. Madame Brenda screeched and held up her hands against the reptile. But the lizard went directly to Alice. Alice put out her hand, mesmerized by the creature. He crawled into her palm and curled up there quite happily. Olivia thought of something then, a hunch. The possibility of a strange coincidence.

"Alice," Olivia said, "you said your husband was a sailor. Where did his ship sail?"

"The last I heard he was in the Mediterranean Ocean, somewhere near the Hydrocophegene Islands."

Olivia nodded. She wasn't surprised. Nothing could surprise her this day.

"Hey, Buster," the lizard said softly.

"Papa," Patrick said. Once again Alice broke into sobs, harder than before. It was then that Olivia told Alice about Sidi. It was a long, strange tale, and at the end Alice gazed down at the lizard.

"So you're saying that this lizard is my husband?" Alice said.

"He might be," Olivia answered.

"Do you suppose," Alice asked Madame Brenda, "that he might, someday, turn back into a human?"

"Darling," said Madame Brenda, "I once had a husband who looked a lot like a weasel. He never stopped looking like a weasel, but after a couple of years I hardly noticed it at all."

Alice nodded at this bit of wisdom. She went to her kitchen cabinet and found an empty mustard jar and put her husband in it.

"Just until I find something more roomy," she whispered to him.

"Hey, Buster," he said agreeably.

"Well," Madame Brenda said, draining the last of her iced tea and standing up. "Looks like I'm finished here. Farewell, darlings. It's been a pleasure."

"But what about my brother?" Olivia said. "You told me you were going to contact my brother."

"I've got a plane to catch tomorrow morning, darling, and what with the shopping and the ghosts I am completely done in." Madame Brenda sighed.

"But that's why I came!" Olivia cried. "Because you are supposed to be so good at talking to spirits. My brother even had your book in his library. And all you did was scribble down a few words on a piece of paper. That's nothing! I think you are a fake, Madame Brenda. A huge fake. Anyone can do what you did!"

"Not anyone," Madame Brenda said. She took both of Olivia's hands in her own. Olivia tried to pull them away, but Madame Brenda was surprisingly strong. "But I believe that *you* can do what I do, Olivia. *You* can talk to spirits too. I see the gift in you . . . in fact, you may be the very person I have been searching for."

"But I can't!" Olivia said. She was crying now. Her body was suddenly exhausted. She wanted to go home. She wanted to climb into bed and pull the covers over her head. "I've *tried* to contact Christopher. Every day I try to get him to talk to me, but I never hear anything at all. Just silence. He left me. He's gone, evaporated. Like steam into the air," she said, using Branwell's words.

"Now, now, don't excite yourself . . . it's very bad for the colon." Madame Brenda opened her pocketbook and said, "I have something for you. I tried to slip it to you under the table, but you were too interested in that slithering lizard to notice." She pulled out the piece of paper on which she had written the ghost's words. "I didn't read everything out loud. At the very end, the spirit sent a special message. It was a message to you, Olivia." Madame

Brenda smiled as she folded the paper up into a little square and pressed it into Olivia's hand.

"So long, dear Alice," Madame Brenda said to her hostess, who was staring down in wonder at the lizard in the mustard jar. "Perhaps I'll see you the next time my shoe sales roll around!"

"Oh, yes, yes. Good-bye, Madame Brenda." Alice waved at her distractedly.

"Remember, darling," Madame Brenda said to Olivia before she departed, "listening to the dead is just like tuning your radio to the right station. At first you might hear a lot of static. But the moment you hear a voice, stop moving the dial. And listen."

Twenty

Olivia looked down at the folded note in her hand. Carefully, hesitantly, she unfolded it. It might simply be another trick of Madame Brenda's. She might have jotted down a little note to Olivia just to make her feel better.

Her eyes passed over the sloppy writing. She looked down at the bottom of the page and read the last sentence: *Can Olivia please meet me down in the subbasement?* She blinked, then read it again, just to be sure. How could Madame Brenda have known about the subbasement? Olivia's mind worked through her suspicions. She had lived in New York City her whole life. It had taught her to be suspicious of everyone.

In the end Olivia decided it was a hoax. A wild-goose chase. But still, to satisfy her own curiosity, she said a hasty good-bye to Alice, kissed Patrick on top of his head, and headed for the subbasement.

She felt brave enough from the eleventh floor to the fifth floor. But when the elevator got closer to the basement, she began to feel slightly queasy. What if someone were waiting for her down there? A criminal maybe. Or even worse, she thought suddenly, a ghost.

She got off at the basement floor, then found the little stairwell that led down. It felt even colder than before. She wished she had taken Branwell with her, then remembered that she was still angry with him for deserting her. Anyway, the message had been for her, and her alone.

At the subbasement door she hesitated, her fingers on the door handle. She thought of Master Clive—his cruelty and his cleverness. She wondered if he had devised this plan, with Madame Brenda in cahoots, to get Olivia to go down to the subbasement alone. And once he got her there, he would put on his black rubber gloves and strangle her, the way he had strangled Delilah's father. The thought chilled Olivia to the bone.

She took her hand off the handle. She would not risk it, she decided. It was too dangerous. She turned to leave, but a sensation came over her. She felt a floating sadness; it was not *her* sadness, but someone else's. It felt like someone was pleading with her to open the subbasement door and go inside. She could say, "No." She could go back up the stairs and up the elevator to her apartment, where the brownies would be warm and waiting. She almost did. Then she turned around and pulled open the door.

A blast of cold air hit her once again. She wished she had brought a sweater. She also wished she had brought a flashlight. The darkness was very thick once the door shut behind her. She stood blinking into the blackness, waiting for her eyes to adjust. Gradually they did and she made out the four corners of the room and the cylindrical shape in the center. But nothing else. The room was perfectly empty. It was as she had first suspected—one of Madame Brenda's tricks.

Olivia walked up to the cylinder and, with her fingertips, traced along the shallow grooves between the bricks. She could smell its musty age. She wondered at all the other hands that had once touched the brick. The hands of the Berns family who had once lived here. Rough, callused hands, she imagined. Hands that were used to hard work and never-ending chores—plowing fields and bundling hay and milking cows. Looking after brothers and sisters.

Then, all of a sudden, Olivia *knew.* She knew! In the darkness she lifted her head and called out in a clear, confident voice, "Branwell."

It took a moment before a quivering circle of bluish

light began to form in front of her. It started small, but gradually stretched and twisted and began to take shape. The color turned from blue to white, and then finally the edges began to grow sharp. The light became more opaque. Olivia watched, with unexpected calmness, as fingers grew out of blobs, and the blobs turned into hands. Rough, callused hands. She looked up at where the head should be. Slowly, facial features emerged as though they were being raised and sculpted by an invisible artist. The nose, the sensitive mouth, the dark eyes with the rounded brows above them. Branwell.

He looked confused. Gazing around him, he bit at his lip—a lip that now was as real and fleshy as Olivia's.

"Is your father gone?" he asked. It was as though he had picked up where they had last left off hours ago, when George Kidney had suddenly appeared in the subbasement. Olivia nodded.

"He's gone," she said. She stared at him. So *this* was a ghost. This person who stood before her, with feelings and thoughts. Who laughed and worried about little Charlie. Who had held her hand. What was the difference between a ghost and a living person? There didn't seem to be any real difference at all. It must be like this for Christopher too—only she just wasn't able to see him the way she could see Branwell. Why? Why? She looked into Branwell's face and once again she saw the trace of confusion. Of sadness. She remembered Madame Brenda's words about ghosts who don't know that they are dead: *"The ones that won't accept it have a hard time. They try to fit into this life, but they can't. People don't see them or hear them. They wind up feeling all alone and they don't know why."*

Olivia put out her hand and touched Branwell's face. His cheek was cold. He smiled at her, changing his expression so that he looked easygoing. Right then Olivia knew exactly how he felt. She had moved around so much, going from school to school, never feeling like she belonged anywhere. And without Christopher she didn't. She was alone. So she faked it. She faked a cool, breezy attitude of someone who did belong. Who was happy. Just like Branwell was doing now.

"You are dead," Olivia said bluntly. Branwell squinted at her, smiled.

"That's news to me," he joked.

"That's the trouble," Olivia said. "You don't know you're dead. But think for a minute. You said you belong to the Biffmeyer family. But your own mother doesn't remember you."

"It's all the kids and animals . . . ," he began uneasily.

"And none of the other Biffmeyer kids seemed to pay any attention to you or to hear what you said to them."

"That's just how they are," he said.

"And you said you're in my English class and you sit next to Wayne, the kid with the . . . with the . . ."

"The boil," Branwell said.

"The boil. Right. But I started to think about that. And I remembered that Wayne sits alone at a double desk. He always has." Branwell was silent at this. The confusion set into his face. It pained Olivia to see him like that. But he *had* to know.

"If I were dead," Branwell said, growing angry, "don't you think I would know it?!"

"I'm not sure," Olivia said. "I'm not sure of anything anymore."

They were silent for a moment. Then Branwell said, "Don't you wonder what this thing is?" He slapped the side of the brick cylinder.

"You're changing the subject," Olivia said. But Branwell suddenly looked so glum and dispirited that she decided to oblige him. And besides, she was curious to know also.

"Okay. If you give me a lift," Olivia said, "I'll try to see what's at the top. Just kneel down. I'm getting up on your shoulders." He knelt down and she carefully stepped up on his shoulders, balancing herself with her hands on top of Branwell's head. He stood up very slowly. But even with the addition of Branwell's height, Olivia could not quite see the top. Still, if she reached up, her hands could almost grip the upper edge of the cylinder. It was risky. The bricks were crumbling badly along the top. If she thought too much about it, she knew that she would chicken out, so with one swift motion, she jumped up from his shoulders and grabbed the lip of the cylinder. It took a great deal of effort, but Olivia managed to pull herself up, swinging first one leg, then the other over the edge until she was sitting on top of the cylinder. Her heart was beating fast and it took her a full moment to recover her wits and inspect the structure. She found that it was not solid all the way through. In the middle of the cylinder was a wide, deep hole. It was so deep, in fact, that she could not see the bottom. She sat up on that high perch for a moment, thinking.

"Branwell," she yelled down to him. "I think I know what this is!"

Twenty-one

"What is it?" Branwell called up to her.

"I'll tell you as soon as I get off this thing." Getting down was harder than going up. She clung to the crumbling edge precariously, her legs dangling while Branwell tried to reach up and grab them. By contrast, her escape from Master Clive's terrace was a piece of cake. Branwell couldn't quite reach her legs, so she would have to let go of the edge, fall, and hope that Branwell caught her. She closed her eyes.

"Are you ready?" she called down to him.

"I'll catch you," he said.

"Okay, here I go." She began to let go. But at the last minute she got scared and tried to grab the edge again. Of course it was too late, and her descent wound up being a clumsy, scraping tumble that Branwell, fortunately, was able to stop before she hit the concrete floor. He put her down on her feet, but she sank to the floor anyway, her back against the brick.

Branwell sat down beside her and gave her a minute to catch her breath before saying, "So what do you think this thing is?"

"I think," Olivia said, inspecting a nasty scrape on her forearm, "that it's a well. An old well that people drew their water from. Probably left over from the farm that used to be on this site."

"The Berns's farm," Branwell said suddenly. He stood up and Olivia stood up too.

"That's right! You knew that! Branwell"—she turned to him—"who's Johnny Berns?" Branwell winced. His body began to get fuzzy around the edges as though he were melting back into that blue light. He was disappearing again.

"No!" Olivia said sternly. "You won't put your fingers in your ears this time! Come back this instant, Branwell, or I will never speak to you again!" The shapeless form began to take shape once again. But he still remained blurry, as though she were seeing him through a thick fog.

"Who is Johnny Berns?" she asked again with great determination.

"Johnny," Branwell said, grunting out the name as if he

had difficulty even saying it, "is my younger brother. He's never where you need him to be. He's always running off. Getting into trouble. He hates the farm. He hates milking the cows and mucking out the barn. He was supposed to help me in the barn today, but now I can't find him."

"What day is it today?" Olivia asked.

"May third," Branwell answered. Olivia put out her hand to touch his hand. She touched cold air instead. He was no longer solid flesh, yet he was still there.

"What year is it?" Olivia asked. There was a short pause.

"1837," Branwell answered. Olivia put her hand on the well, just to reassure herself with something solid. Something real. Yet the well was also from the lost, distant past. With the cold brick beneath her hand Olivia considered that the well was a link between the past and the present. It gave Olivia and Branwell the same feeling of sadness, the same feeling that something had happened here.

"Did you come to the well to look for Johnny?" Olivia asked suddenly.

"Yes."

"Did you find him?"

"Yes," Branwell said. His voice sounded like it was coming from a long distance away.

"What was he doing?" Olivia asked.

"He had fallen into the well. He couldn't get out. There was nothing for him to grab on to. He didn't cry out for help. He'd gotten into trouble so many times that he didn't want our parents to know he was in trouble again."

"What did you do?"

"I tried to get him. I let out the bucket rope and climbed down. But the rope wasn't strong enough. It broke and I fell in too."

"Then what happened?" Olivia asked quietly. There was no answer for a very long time. Light pulsated through his cloudy body, like the beat of a heart.

"What happened, Branwell?" Olivia repeated.

"We drowned. Both of us."

"Oh, Branwell." The hazy shape of Branwell's body began to thin out and dissolve into the air until finally he was completely gone and Olivia was once again alone.

Twenty-two

With a heavy heart, Olivia rode the elevator back up to the twelfth floor. She wondered if she had done the right thing in making Branwell see that he was dead. When he had realized he was a ghost, his voice had sounded so sad. Now Branwell was gone. Just like Christopher. Before, at least, she was able to see Branwell. She was able to talk to him. He was so easy to talk to and had been good company. A friend. But it was useless to think about it. And besides, now Branwell wouldn't have to pretend to be a Biffmeyer child. He wouldn't be frustrated and confused and always looking for something without finding it. She knew how that felt.

The twelfth floor smelled strongly of brownies. She realized, for the first time, how much she and her father relied on each other. And how lucky it was that they *did* have each other.

No sooner had she thought about that than the door to apartment 12K opened and Princepessa Christina Lilli's old friend and servant appeared. Not surprisingly, she was carrying her tremendous garbage can, full of dirty air, no doubt. When she saw Olivia, she stopped and said, "You again?! Don't you have a home to go to?"

"Yes, and I'm going there right now, for your information," Olivia said tartly. She was not really mad, but she pretended to be. Olivia guessed that the woman liked rudeness in other people. Maybe, Olivia thought, it's because she misses Princepessa Christina Lilli, who sounded very spoiled and rude indeed.

"And I suppose that filthy smell is coming from your apartment?" The little lady had put her garbage can down and planted her bony fingers on her hips.

"If you mean the smell of brownies, yes it is."

"Hmmm. I don't care for brownies," the woman said.

"Then you won't want to come to my home and have some," Olivia said. She turned her back to the woman and began to walk toward her apartment.

"And who are you to decide what *I* want, young lady?! You are very impertinent. I think I will go to your apartment right now and have a little talk with your parents. Tell them what a saucy, impertinent girl you are. They will be sure to punish you severely."

"Well?" Olivia stopped, waited. "Are you coming or not?" The little woman scurried off to empty her dirty air in the incinerator and then put the garbage can back in her house. She reappeared a few moments later. She had tidied up her hair and applied fresh lipstick.

"You look nice," Olivia said.

"Thank you," she said with great dignity.

George Kidney was a silly man but he was no fool. He took one look at the little lady and bowed deeply. He took her hand and kissed it, which was exactly the right thing to do. The woman complimented him on his fine manners and told him that he had a lovely daughter and that she simply adored brownies.

They all sat together at the dining room table, nibbling on brownies and drinking milk, and it looked to be a very sociable evening. George Kidney said he was glad to finally meet one of his neighbors.

"Apartment life always seems so strange to me," George said. "Everyone is all stacked up on top of each other and yet no one knows anyone else."

"It's barbaric!" the little woman declared. "Where I

come from . . ." She stopped abruptly and touched her face. George and Olivia looked at her. Her complexion had suddenly turned pink and splotchy.

"Oh, my," she said. She looked down at the half-eaten brownie on her plate. "Were there any walnuts in the brownies?"

"Loads of them," Olivia said.

"Oh, my." Her face was going from pink to red. "I am allergic to walnuts."

"What can we do?" George asked.

"Just bring me a cool, damp washcloth, please." They led her to the couch, where she lay down, and George dabbed a cool washcloth against her face. All the while Olivia was thinking. And wondering.

After a few moments the woman sat up. Her skin looked clearer. She seemed a little embarrassed, but George chattered on about all the people he knew with allergies to strawberries and chocolate and lobster and rice pudding, and just as he had nearly exhausted his list, Olivia piped up and said, "Excuse me. Can I ask you a question?"

"I suppose." The woman eyed Olivia suspiciously.

"I'm beginning to think that *you* are the Princepessa Christina Lilli."

"That is not a question," the woman said haughtily.

"You said that the Princepessa Christina Lilli was very allergic to walnuts."

"And so am I," the woman said, her voice rising.

"And you have her jewelry," Olivia continued.

"Only a very little bit of it."

"You didn't answer my question," Olivia persisted.

"And you didn't ask it."

"All right then," Olivia said. "Are you the Princepessa Christina Lilli?"

"Yes, I am!" There was a moment of absolute silence, which was finally broken by George Kidney.

"Would Her Highness like another glass of milk?" he asked carefully.

Twenty-three

"But how did you escape from the soldiers who took you and your family away?" Olivia asked.

"Oh, it wasn't difficult," the Princepessa said. "They were stupid brutes and it was easy to trick them into stopping before we got to the prison in Refnastova. Once we were out of the truck, we all fought them, but I was the only one who got away. I could run very fast back then, and I dashed into the deep woods where they couldn't find me.

"I spent several days walking and walking. I wondered if I would ever come out of those woods. They seemed to stretch on forever. But one day the forest ended and I found myself in a town that I knew quite well. We had a wealthy cousin, Baron Von Shrift, who lived in that very town. I went to him for help and he chartered a ship for me. It had to be done under the greatest cloak of secrecy.

So many people hated the royal family back then. You never knew who might betray you.

"I boarded the ship even before the crew did. Me and what little belongings I had managed to sew into my dress. I never once came out of my room. No one knew who I was. I took all my meals in the cabin. Although the SS *Rosenquist* was one of the most luxurious ships of that time, I might have been sailing in a wooden crate for all I saw of it."

"You sailed on the SS *Rosenquist*?" Olivia was shocked to hear the name of the grand ship for the second time that day.

"Didn't I just say that?" The Princepessa was back to her old, snappish self again. "Take the wax out of your ears."

"*You* were the mysterious passenger," Olivia said. "But how did you escape Master Clive?"

"Master Clive?" The Princepessa seemed to be searching her memory for the name. "Ah, do you mean that ridiculous pirate fellow? He found me in my cabin while he was searching for valuables. And yes, he did bore me for a while with his threats and nonsense, but I finally put an end to that."

"How?"

"I slapped him smartly. And I told him that his gloves were very tacky. After that we sailed along quite peacefully until he saw me safely aboard a freighter bound for New York City."

"You are an astonishing woman, Princepessa Christina Lilli," George Kidney said respectfully.

"Of course I am," she agreed. She handed George her empty glass and stood up in her little white shoes. "And we will keep this little secret between ourselves, won't we?"

"But now that you're safe from your enemies," Olivia persisted, "why can't you just admit that you are the Princepessa?"

"Safe from my enemies?! Hmmph! Why, no one is more faithful than an enemy. You may lose your friends, but your enemies will never abandon you. Good night." Then she turned to George and said, "You may visit me whenever you like. And as for you, you insolent, young savage," she said to Olivia, "I shall expect you for Poor Richard's tarts and Cambrian tea tomorrow at three-thirty sharp."

Twenty-four

Olivia went to bed early that night. She lay there, listening to the sound of cars passing on the street below, driven by strangers, people she would never meet. Still, the world suddenly seemed very small. People were connected in the strangest ways, ways that they couldn't always see themselves. It made her feel less alone. But what about Branwell? He was always worried about everyone else. Now Olivia was worried about him. Was he scared? Was he alone?

She closed her eyes, and her thoughts naturally turned toward Christopher. He loved chaos. "Life is messy," Christopher used to say. "It's noisy and there are too many people and it sometimes smells bad . . . but I'm never bored." Olivia hoped that wherever he was, it was just as messy and chaotic. She hoped that, occasionally, it even smelled bad.

Suddenly Olivia became aware of a quiet buzzing in the room. It had a high whining pitch that sounded electronic. She thought it might be her alarm clock, but that was way over on her desk. The buzzing sounded like it was right next to her ear. After a moment it began to change pitch and grow more piercing. Then it plummeted to a dull static, like a radio that was between stations. She opened her eyes and listened harder. After a moment she detected, beneath the static, the faint sound of a voice. It came and went and she could not make out any words. But still she kept listening. After a while, the static subsided and the voice began to emerge. It was exactly as Madame Brenda had described it—like adjusting the dials on a radio until you could get a station.

"Hello?" the voice said.

"Hello," Olivia answered. She kept her voice very soft. She did not want her father to hear.

"Olivia?" the voice asked.

"Oh, Christopher!" Olivia replied. Tears were pooling in her eyes—tears of joy. She looked all around her dimly lit room, but she couldn't see him the way she was able to see Branwell. "Why didn't you talk to me before?"

"I tried," Christopher said. "I never got an answer."

"Me too."

"I guess we were both dialing the wrong number, kiddo. Hey, I can see you now. You're a little fuzzy but I can see you. You cut your hair."

"Last week. I hate it."

"It looks good on you."

"Christopher?" She couldn't stop smiling now, any more

than she could have stopped her own heart from beating. Even though she couldn't see him, she felt him in a way that was stronger than seeing him. "Christopher, where are you?"

"Well," Christopher said after a pause, "let's see. Where do you go when you dream?"

Olivia thought about that for a minute. She imagined a place that had no name, that shifted and changed. A place populated with people whom you seemed to know, but couldn't quite remember how.

"Okay, I guess I can picture it," Olivia said. "Is that what it's like there?"

"Something like that."

"Christopher, I miss you so much." Then a thought occurred to her: maybe she really *was* crazy. And the voice that she heard was not Christopher's at all but a symptom of madness. She thought about her day. It was so bizarre, what with Master Clive and Sidi and Madame Brenda. Maybe it was all in her mind. Just like Renee had said—if a person were crazy, they probably wouldn't even know it. What if none of it had really happened? What if her mind was just telling her lies? Ms. Dart was a professional. She said Olivia might need medication. Maybe she was right.

"No, Olivia," Christopher said. "You're not crazy. You see, you don't have to speak out loud for me to hear you. I can hear what you are thinking. So you can stop trying to talk to me while you're in school . . . that just freaks people out. Oh, boy, I can see that you still don't believe me. You still think that maybe this is your mind talking. Okay, kiddo. You want proof? You know Dad's old wooden toolbox? The one Grandpa gave him when he was a kid? He keeps it hidden on the top shelf of the coat closet. When we're finished here, go and open that old toolbox up."

"Why?" Olivia asked. Only now she didn't bother to say it out loud, she just thought it.

"Oh, for Pete's sake, Olivia, just do it! Sheesh. I can see you haven't changed at all. Which reminds me. A funny thing happened today. I was having a conversation with this guy, telling him that my sister was the most first-rate kid on the planet. And this guy says he bets he knows someone even more first-rate. And we have this great big argument until finally he says, 'I don't care what you say. As far as I'm concerned, there isn't anyone more first-rate than Olivia Kidney.' How do you like that? We were both talking about the same person."

"Branwell!" Olivia thought.

"Yup, that was his name. I knew it was something with *bran* in it. Decent guy."

"Very. Tell him hi for me."

"Sure thing. Listen, kiddo, I'm sure you're busy these days, but how about we check in with each other now and then, okay? Now that we know how to find each other. And don't forget about the toolbox."

"I won't. Bye, Christopher." She said this out loud. Just to hear the words.

"Later, kiddo."

She didn't move for a few minutes. The buzzing was gone. The feeling of Christopher was gone too. But not completely.

She got out of bed and left her room. Her father was sleeping. She could hear him snoring softly in his bedroom. She tiptoed down the hall to the coat closet and opened the door. Inside was a mess of coats and windbreakers, all squeezed together on hangers. Above the hangers was a shelf that was likewise crammed full. Olivia pulled over a chair to stand on so she could examine the shelf more closely. The shelf was heaped with junk—old shoe boxes and broken umbrellas, three board games that she never knew they had, a tin of bent nails, a waffle iron, and, way in the back, hidden behind her father's bunched-up work coveralls, the old wooden toolbox.

She vaguely remembered the toolbox. Her father had loved it, but Olivia's mother had hated it. She said it made George look very unprofessional. One year she bought George a brand-new, fire-engine-red toolbox to replace the old wooden one. George knew that if his wife gave him a new toolbox, he would have to use it. Since then, Olivia had never seen the old wooden one.

Olivia grabbed the toolbox and put it on the floor, then sat down cross-legged in front of it. She took a breath, flipped the latch, and slowly opened the lid.

"Oh!" she said. She stared, smiled. Inside, carefully arranged side by side, were the two dolls that Christopher had hidden all those years ago. The brother and sister dolls. The two small faces stared up at her, faces eerily similar to Christopher's and her own. Their lips were both slightly turned up, as though Olivia had caught them just as they'd heard a pretty good joke. Not hilarious, but really pretty good all the same. They were safe. They were fine. And so was she.